Towards Quality Education in India

Towards Quality Education in India

Study and Training Material for Teachers, Instructors and Education Administrators

Dr. Binodanand Jha

PRABHAT PRAKASHAN
ISO 9001: 2015 Publishers

Published by
PRABHAT PRAKASHAN
4/19 Asaf Ali Road,
New Delhi-110 002 (INDIA)
e-mail: prabhatbooks@gmail.com

ISBN 978-93-5322-467-7
TOWARDS QUALITY EDUCATION IN INDIA
by Dr. Binodanand Jha

Edition
First, 2019

Price
₹ 300.00 (Rupees Three Hundred only)

Printed at
R-Tech Offset Printers, Delhi

Qualitative Education is Possible through Multidimensional Efforts

Budha and Gandhi, the two great men, have intimate relation with Bihar. Generally all educational functions in Bihar are inaugurated with the name of Budha and Gandhi but sadly only taking their name is considered to be the fulfilment of our duty. Gandhi took illiteracy as the cause of poverty, exploitation, backwardness in Champaran. He established first school at Badharwa Lakhansen—35 kms from Motihari in November 1917 from 08.11.1917 to 19.11.1917. Administration of this school was entrusted by Gandhiji to Baban Gokhale, an engineer who came from Bombay (Mumbai), his wife Avantika Bai Gokhale and the younger son of Gandhiji – Devdas Gandhi. After about century every Panchayat and every Village in Bihar has got schools and their proximity ensured for every house. Teachers are selected from the same locality. Building, infrastructure, mid day meal, free books, uniform etc. are easily available. Despite all efforts, imparting quality education is a challenge. Average attendance of the children in the State is 60 to 65 percent and we are not successful in imparting qualitaty education. More efforts are to be made for converting Education into Education for All.

The first question is: who owns the school? The Government and Administration cannot be absolved from their responsibility but the thought that School is only of

Education Department will not strengthen our belief in Sarva Shiksha or Education for All. Teachers, guardians, People's representatives, Panchayat, Village and everybody should feel that this School is ours then only we can move ahead with greater strength. Teachers have got many problems which are to be resolved sensibly and with priority. Our Offices should be determined to serve them, they should have improved work environment; if teachers are aggrieved, conscious about their rights and their angry attitude becomes hurdle in imparting education how will the students reach the stage of *Gurave Namah*?

Children at Government School are mostly from socially, economically and educationally backward strata of the society. Some parents may be illiterate or they being busy in arranging the livelihood are not able to assist and support their children in learning. We will have to take special care of such Children. Imparting education to weak children should be taken as a challenge.

For tackling the problem of learning language we have initiated a programme named 'Padho Purvi Champaran' as an experiment in the five blocks of Purvi Champaran. This programme has been a remarkably successful; such a campaign is to be taken to other divisions also. Teacher are to be positively strengthened with which the entire class room system is to be made so effective that in the coming years children naturally come up in the Language-Mathematics subjects in accordance with the class.

With the advent of modernity, negativism is also creeping in the society. Indisciplined freedom in place of freedom, violence in place of peace and disrespect to elderly and women are evident in our society. Only few are keen on living with dedication, morality and simplicity. Cunningness and if need be earning profit by flouting rules are very common. With such tendencies education with values is no longer useful for the society. The family and school will have to take proper initiative in the last few years the disturbances connected with distribution of amount for uniforms, scholarships and bicycles have posed a question mark on the role of two institutions namely family and school. In the old days even by taking teacher's name we were able to regulate child's tantrums—our behaviour used to be regulated only with the mention of the teacher's name. Days changed and in this decade if the child does any mischief parents are called to the school, but presently the importance of both these institutions have lowered down. During the distribution of Bicycles and Uniforms in certain schools students misbehaved with teachers and even took to vandalism. At few places teachers also flouted the rules and disregarded the teacher – student relationship. These problems call for serious thinking and regulated behaviour on our part.

In education, repetition of things, mugging, memorizing without knowing the 'artha' is not helpful in creation of an educated society. In teaching learning process understanding and analysis are to be given prime place. Atmosphere needs to be created for raising questions in the class room. Questions should be asked if the topic is not understood. Liberal freedom should also be there for students to question the teacher's views as well the contents of books. There should be room for disagreement; new investigations and innovations should be in place for constructive arguments.

Up to yesterday teachers were in the centre of education but now the students are in the centre. Now teachers cannot move with punishment and extreme strictness. Today there is no relation between age and knowledge. With the explosion of facts and information nobody can claim that by virtue of age or born earlier he knows more. Now the things will move with courtesy and humbleness. Now the new teacher cannot be student's father. He should prepare himself in the role of elder brother/sister or friend who will facilitate and encourage the child. The knowledge acquired in this environment will travel long distance with the student. Teacher will develop shared understanding with which knowledge will be created.

In this book essays, practices and contributions relating to quality education are provided to the teachers. With these articles we have made efforts to raise the level of quality education, but it seems a very small and tiny effort. Most of the questions have remained unanswered. Through this book my effort is to study, debate and form views to insure the continuity of progress. Thinking—pondering is necessary but final conclusion is to give effective shape to dreams, principles and views. The saying by Buddha that "**You may speak or write any number of pious words but up to when they are not followed they have no benefit or value is significant**". Let us make a forceful and effective trial.

The articles in this book are taken from various sources, writers and poets to all of them I extend hearty gratitude. I take this opportunity to express my thankfulness to Dr. Subodh Kumar Jha, Associate Professor & Head, Dept. of English, S.N.S. College, Jehanabad for going through the manuscript and making value additions. Dr. Jha has been a constant support to this endeavour. With all good wishes.

—Dr. Binodanand Jha

Contents

Mahatma Gandhi's View About Education

—R.K. Prabhu and U.R. Rao

An old saying *"Sa Vidya Ya Vimuktaye"* is as true today as it was earlier. Here education does not mean only spiritual education nor 'Vimukti' means 'Moksha' after death. Knowledge contains all trainings which are important services to the human force and 'Vimukti' means coming out of all the dependence in one's life. Dependence can be of two types : slavery to external factors and man's slavery to artificial requirements. Acquisition of Knowledge for achieving such ideal is true education.

Knowledge for Living

In present days pure water, pure soil and pure air have become unfamiliar for us. We do not know the supreme value of sky and sun. If we use diligently the five factors namely Earth, Water, Sky, Fire, Air and take balanced food we will be able to complete the desired work. For attaining such knowledge neither degrees nor crores of rupees are required. For this dedication toward God, enthusiasms to serve, introduction to five 'tatvas' and knowledge of what is to be eaten are important. These can be achieved without wasting time in school and college.

Continuous doubt and pure inquisitiveness are the first condition for acquisition of knowledge. In the spirit of inquisitiveness, humble approach and respect toward teacher should be evident. Beware that it is not converted into indiscipline. Indiscipline is averse to acceptability of mental status. Without humbleness and desire to learn, acquiring knowledge is impossible. For creating a new world, education should also be new. A man becomes man not by literacy or excellence but by education required for true life.

It is my request that before adult's right to vote, earlier arrangements be made for popular education which should necessarily not based on books, as books possibly can play helper's role. It is my belief that English Education has made our mind like skeleton and weak which never prefer that supports a courageous nationality. I will provide them adequate knowledge through capable languages on which any country feels proud. If honesty and enthusiasm is there the insight of nationality can be learned in a short time.

Importance of Labour

It is my belief that because majority of our time goes in efforts required for employment and food. Our children should be taught importance of labour. Our teaching to them should not be in a way projecting labour as an inferior thing. There should not be any reason which in present days is evident that the son of a farmer after going to school be not inclined to work as an agricultural helper.

Bookish Education should follow Labour Education (meant for laborious activities). Hands are given by nature to human beings which distinguish them from Animals. It is Andhviswas that without knowing the art of reading and writing man's absolute development is not possible. Though this is correct that by knowing reading-writing, life takes a larger shape but this cannot be taken without alternative for a man's moral and physical development in any form.

It is my belief that true education relating to mind can be only through putting exercises and its training on hands, legs, eyes, ears, nose and other organs of body. In other words teaching a child, the diligent use of his or her body's organs is the best method of developing mind in the fastest and perfect manner, but alongwith the mind and body the soul should also be awakened otherwise the development will be one sided. I intend spiritual teaching as teaching of heart. So the development of mind and wisdom can only be achieved when simultaneous integrated approach is taken for physical and spiritual teachings/education. They are undivided units. Therefore, by this principle it is misleading that the development can be done in parts or independently from each other. Because of lack of proper coordination between Body, Mind and Soul the good results are not evident which can be seen around us. We are not aware of them because of Vikrit Sahcharya.

A man is not only mind, not only perishable body nor heart and soul, but is also a perfect combination of all the three and this should be included in the correct planning after Education.

The meaning taken by me for education is that which can convert and boost what is best in the child as well as man's personality, mind and soul. Literacy is neither the end of education nor its beginning. It is only a method of teaching man and woman. Literacy in itself is not education. Therefore I will start teaching a child useful handwork (dastkari) and will make effort that he makes something from the beginning. I feel that by adopting such system of education greater development of mind and soul can be developed to a greater extent. It has to be kept in mind that the teaching of handicraft should not be mechanical, but with scientific procedure so that every child is able to know what it has been done. I give more importance to cultural aspect than to literary aspect.

With intelligence the doing of useful physical labour is the best source for development of mind. Coordinated development of body, mind and soul can only develop a balanced mind—the mind which emerges because of sociable labour will become tool for service and it will not easily be misled on wrong paths.

New Education

One who testifies to the 'sarvabhaumikta' can only become medium for basic handwork training. Handwork, Art, Health and Education be integrated in one plan. New Education is a beautiful mixture of these four which contains complete education of a man right from conceivement of a child up to death. I consider handicraft and Industry as medium for Education.

My new education does not depend on money. Expenses incurred may be earned from the education procedure that whatever may be criticism of this but, I know education is education when it is self dependent.

This is known as new policy of Education because it is neither imported from foreign nor it is imposed by them, rather suitable to the Indian Environment which has got rural orientation. It believes in balance between body, mind and soul with which man is made. It is not like western education in which importance is primarily attached to materialism necessitating attention toward body and mind but soul is neglected. The best way to provide education is through handicraft. New Education (Nai Taleem)'s second importance is that it is absolutely self dependent. Therefore to run this, crores of rupees are not required.

What teacher takes is his earning. New Education System is supportive of art of living. Therefore both teacher and student have to produce something during the process of teaching and learning. This makes life rich from the beginning. This saves Nation from searching jobs. This education system develops all the three—mind, body and soul. In comparison to this the general education system pays attention only to mind.

People generally name this as Education through handicraft, which is true but it is only a portion of truth. In fact the roots of new education goes deeper than that. In all areas of human-process they have gone up to the usage of truth and love. Education through Handicraft is attached to the fact that activities of life should be full with truth and love. The aspiration of love is that correct education should be available to all; it be useful to all villagers too in their day to day life. Such education neither be taken from books nor dependent on them. It has got no relation with particular religious section. If at all they are connected with any religion it is the religion for all (Sarvabhaum), out of which all religious sects have come out. Therefore this education is learned from life's book having no cost, which also cannot be snatched by any might of the world.

Education at University

Education at Universities should be aimed at preparing true servants for the Country who live and die for Country's Independence. Therefore my view is that university education should be coordinated with basic education and it be in the same framework. As far as women's education is concerned, I am not sure as to when it should start and be different from men's education, but it is my firm opinion that women should get equal facilities and whenever required special facilities be given.

I am never a supporter of our students going abroad. It has been my experience that after coming back they find it difficult to cope up with the environment here. Valuable experience is one which can contribute maximum to the Country's prosperity.

Code for Students

Joining any Movement or Agitation is meant for those

who have completed their studies. During the course of study sole work and aim of a student is to enlarge their knowledge. Many types of education provided in the Country should be for progress.

Most important is that students should be polite and of good habits, greatest is one who on his own occupy the lowest position. As per Hindu Mythology the life of a student up to completion of education—should be of a` Sanyasi. He cannot marry nor can indulge in indecency. He can not take drugs. And his behaviour should be of an ideal person having controlled patience.

Medium of Education

With the wrong Indianisation crores of students are continuously suffering the maximum, everyday I am seeing examples of that. We are under the impression that nobody can become 'Boss' without knowing English. Nothing can be more blind a faith than this. No Japanese will be so as we are in this view of ours.

Medium of instruction should be changed immediately and the regional languages should be given their due place. It may be that with this there may be dislocation in the higher education but that will be a less harm than the grave waste continuing today.

For enhancing dignity and market value of regional languages I would like that Courts in a particular State should use language of the State. Legislative Assemblies/Councils should use language of the State and if more than one language is popular all of them can be used. In the Centre Hindustani language should have top most position.

In my view this question may not be left to the learned for decision. When Country actually will become independent the answer to the question relating to medium of instruction will be this only. Learned people's work will be to make curriculum and text books in accordance to that. Only then you will see that students completing education in Independent India will be responsive to Country's requirements. I am afraid that till such time we the educated people ponder with such questions we will not be able to make our free and healthy India as dreamed. With hard efforts we will have to break bonds of slavery, be it educational bond, economical, social or political. Three fourth of the fight is` contained in efforts.

I do not have any doubt that those, in whose hands youngsters' education is, if they want to take decision will find that mother tongue is so required for mental development as mother's milk is for Child's body and health. Child learns first lesson from Mother. Therefore for mental development of a child imposing any language other than mother tongue—to me it is sin against mother land.

National Language

I am requesting ousting of English culturally ill occupied as we have successfully ousted the unrightfully English people's political rule. English Language will have its natural place in commercial and diplomatic channels as international language.

If regional languages are to flourish, Provinces and States are to be rearranged/reconstituted accordingly. Hindustani will be national language but it cannot take place of a regional language. It cannot become medium of instruction in Provinces—but English too cannot be. Its work is to assist States to know their relations with India.

English Language

Maximum development of Indian folk should be without knowledge of English. It is my considered view that the English language which is taught here has weakened the Indians who have studied English. Immense pressure has been developed on the muscular energy of Indian students and it has made us copycat. No country can become a Nation by producing a good number of translators.

Literature

Don't think that I am criticizing English or its vast literature. The writings in 'Harijan' are the proof of my love but as India can not take advantage of cool climate and scenery of England, its vast literature is also of no use to India. India has to grow in its own climate, scenery and literature which may be less than England's climate and literature. We ourselves and our children have to develop on our own legacy. If we follow the legacy of others we will lose ours. We can not flourish eating grain and food provided by others.

I would like that we should read excellent literature of English and other languages of the world through Indian Languages. I am not required to learn Bengali for enjoying Ravindranath's creations. I can study them through translated pieces. Gujarati boys and girls are not required to learn Russian language for enjoying Tolstoy's short stories. They can read them through good translations. Englishmen are proud that world's best literature is available to them translated in English within a week of its publication, then why for reading Shakespeare and Milton's literature I am required to learn English.

□

Philosophy of Education

—Swami Vivekanand

Knowing is Unveiling

Education is the manifestation of the perfection already in man. Knowledge is inherent in man, no knowledge comes from outside; it is all inside. What we say a man 'Knows', should, in strict psychological language, be what he 'discovers' or 'unveils'. What a man 'learns' is really what he 'discovers' by taking the cover off his own soul, which is a mine of infinite knowledge. We say Newton discovered gravitation. Was it sitting anywhere in a corner waiting for him? It was in his own mind; the time came and he found it out. All knowledge that the world has ever received comes from the mind; the infinite library of the universe is in your own mind. The external world is simply the suggestion, the occasion, which sets you to study your own mind. The falling of an apple gave the suggestion to Newton, and he studied his own mind. He rearranged all the previous links of thought in his mind and discovered a new link among them, which we call the law of gravitation. It was not in the apple nor in anything in the centre of the earth.

All Knowledge is Within

All knowledge, therefore, secular or spiritual, is in the

human mind. In many cases it is not discovered, but remains covered, and when the covering is being slowly taken off, we say 'we are learning', and the advance of knowledge is made by the advance of this process of uncovering. The man from whom this veil is being lifted is the more knowing man; the man upon whom it lies thick is ignorant; and the man from whom it has entirely gone is all-knowing, omniscient. Like fire in "a piece of flint", knowledge exists in the mind; suggestion is the friction which brings it out. All knowledge and all power are within. What we call powers, secrets of Nature, and force are all within. All knowledge comes from the human soul. Man manifests knowledge, discovers it within himself, which is pre-existing, through eternity.

Infinite Power is in the Soul

No one was ever really taught by another. Each of us has to teach himself. The external teacher offers only the suggestion which arouses the internal teacher to work to understand things. Then things will be made clearer to us by our own power of perception and thought, and we shall realise them in our own souls. The whole of the big banyan tree which covers acres of ground was in the little seed which was perhaps no bigger than one-eighth of a mustard seed. All that mass of energy was there confined. The gigantic intellect, we know, lies coiled up in the protoplasmic cell. It may seem like a paradox, but it is true. Each one of us has come out of one protoplasmic cell, and all the powers we possess were coiled up there. You cannot say they came from food, for if you heap up food mountains high, what power comes out of it? The energy was there, potentially no doubt, but still there. So is infinite power in the soul of man whether he knows it or not. Its manifestation is only a question of being conscious of it.

The Cask of Glass

The Light Divine within is obscured in most people. It is like a lamp in a cask of iron: no gleam of light can shine through. Gradually, by purity and unselfishness, we can make the obscuring medium less and less dense, until at last it becomes as transparent as glass. Sri Ramakrishna was like the iron cask transformed into a glass cask, through which can be seen the inner light as it is.

Self-education

You cannot teach a child any more than you can grow a plant. The plant develops its own nature. The child also teaches itself. But you can help it to go forward in its own way. What you can do is not of a positive nature but negative. You can take away the obstacles, and knowledge comes out of its own nature. Loosen the soil a little, so that it may come out easily. Put a hedge round it; see that it is not killed by anything. You can supply the growing seed with the materials for the making up of its body, bringing to it the earth, the water, the air that it wants. And there your work stops. It will take all that it wants by its own nature. So with the education of the child. A child educates himself. The teacher spoils everything by thinking that he is teaching. Within man is all knowledge, and it requires only an awakening, and that much is the work of the teacher. We have only to do so much for the boys that they may learn to apply their own intellect to the proper use of their hands, legs, ears and eyes.

Free Growth

That system which aims at educating our boys in the same manner as that of the man who battered his ass, being advised that it could thereby be turned into a horse, should be abolished. Owing to undue domination exercised by the parents, our boys do not get free scope for growth. In every one there are infinite tendencies which require proper scope for satisfaction. Violent attempts at reform always end by retarding reform. If you do not allow one to become a lion, one will become a fox.

Positive Ideas

We should give positive ideas. Negative thoughts only weaken men. Do you not find that where parents are constantly taxing their sons to read and write, telling them that they will never learn anything and calling them fools and so forth, the latter do actually turn out to be so in many cases? If you speak kind words to them and encourage them, they are bound to improve in time. If you can give them positive ideas, people will grow up to be men and learn to stand on their own legs. In language and literature, in poetry and arts, in everything we must point out not the mistakes that people are making in their thoughts and actions, but the way in which they will be able to do these things better. The teaching must be modified according to the needs of the taught. Past lives have moulded our tendencies, and so give to the pupil according to his tendencies. Take every one where he stands and push him forward. We have seen how Sri Ramakrishna would encourage even those whom we considered worthless and change the very course of their lives thereby! He never destroyed a single man's special inclinations. He gave words of hope and encouragement even to the most degraded of persons and lifted them up.

Service as Worship

Liberty is the first condition of growth. It is wrong, a thousand times wrong, if any of you dares to say, 'I will work out the salvation of this woman or child.' Hands off! They will solve their own problems. Who are you to assume that you know everything? How dare you think that you have the right over God? For, don't you know that every soul is the Soul of God? Look upon every one as God. You can only serve. Serve the children of the Lord if you have the privilege. If the Lord grants that you can help any one of His children, blessed you are. Blessed you are that that privilege was given to you when others had it not. Do it only as worship.

Assimilation of Ideas

Education is not the amount of information that is put into your brain and runs riot there, undigested all your life. We must have life-building, man-making, character-making, assimilation of ideas. If you have assimilated five ideas and made them your life and character, you have more education than any man who has got by heart a whole library. If education were identical with information, the libraries would be the greatest sages in the world and encyclopaedias the rishis.

Wrong Education

Getting by heart the thoughts of others in a foreign language and stuffing your brain with them and taking some university degrees, you consider yourself educated. Is this education? What is the goal of your education? Either a clerkship, or being a lawyer, or at the most a Deputy Magistrate, which is another form of clerkship—isn't that all? What good will it do you or to the country at large? Open your eyes and see what a piteous cry for food is rising in the land of Bharata, proverbial for its food. Will your education fulfil this want? The education that does not help the common mass of people to equip themselves for the struggle for life, which does not bring out strength of character, a spirit of philanthropy and the courage of a lion—is it worth the name?

The Needed Education

We want that education by which character is formed, strength of mind is increased, the intellect is expanded and by which one can stand on one's own feet. What we need is to study, independent of foreign control, different branches of the knowledge that is our own, and with it the English language and western science; we need technical education and all else that will develop industries, so that men, instead of seeking for service, may earn enough to provide for themselves and save against a rainy day.

The Goal of Man-making

The end of all education, all training, should be man-making. The end and aim of all training is to make the man grow. The training by which the current and expression of will are brought under control and become fruitful, is called education. What our country now wants are muscles of iron and nerves of steel, gigantic wills which nothing can resist, which can penetrate into the mysteries and secrets of the universe and will accomplish their purpose in any fashion, even if it meant going down to the bottom of the ocean, meeting death face to face. It is man-making religion that we want. It is man-making theories that we want. It is man-making education all round that we want.

□

What will not be Allowed in My School

—**Gijubhai**

If the walls of my School are not white washed and beautiful we will let go

But if there is a Makadi Ka Jala or dust we will not let go

If the Building of my School is not made of grand bricks we will let go

But if Courtyard of School is having rotten holes and the plaster on walls without ash we will not let go

If my School is not having Big Library containing books we will let go

But if even by borrowing the books from others nothing is read or studied it will not be permitted

If carpets are not in the School we will let go

But if dust or garbage is below our legs it will not be permitted

If apparatus/es are not available in my School we will let go

But if few apparatus/es available in my School are not used it will not be permitted

If my School is not having big Children's Library we will let go

But if even handwritten books with enthusiastic features are not there it will not be permitted.

If in my School I am not very learned it can be let go.

But if I am not having respect for boys and girls studying knowing fully well their progress it cannot be allowed

In my School if I don't run for teaching boys and girls, every minute trying to teach them – it will suffice

But if I become hurdle in their work, reprimanding them off and on for studies it will not be permitted.

In my School children's study two minutes and play two minutes it will be permitted

But if work whole day like workers in a Factory and I keep vigilant eyes on them – it will not be permitted.

In my School if children's becoming my friend walk beyond me this can be permitted.

But if Children are afraid of me it will not be permitted.

In my School if children study less, study slowly it will suffice

But if they study in loud voice and get bored with that it will not be permitted.

In my School children's may sit as they want, if they desire can study or make pictures it will be permitted

But if they write or make picture for showing somebody it will not be permitted

Give Us A Role Model

—A.P.J. Abdul Kalam

Why should I meet young students in particular? Seeking the answer I went back to my student days. From the island of Rameswaram, what a great journey it's been! Looking back it all seems quite incredible. What was it that made it possible? Hard work? Ambition? Many things come to my mind. I feel the most important thing was that I always assessed my worth by the value of my contribution. The fundamental thing is that you must know that you deserve the good things of life, the benefits that God bestows. Unless our students and youth believe that they are worthy of being citizens of a developed India, how will they ever be responsible and enlightened citizens?

There is nothing mysterious about the abundance in developed nations. The historic fact is that the people of these nations—the G8 as they are called—believed over many generations that they must live a good life in a strong and prosperous nation. The reality became aligned with their aspirations.

I do not think that abundance and spirituality are mutually exclusive or that it is wrong to desire material things. For instance, while I personally cherish a life with minimum of possessions, I admire abundance, for it brings along with it security and confidence, and these eventually help preserve our freedom. Nature too does not do anything by half measures, as you will see if you look around you. Go to a garden. In season, there is a profusion of flowers. Or look up. The universe stretches into infinitude, vast beyond belief.

All that we see in the world is an embodiment of energy. We are a part of the cosmic energy too, as Sri Aurobindo says. Therefore when we begin to appreciate that spirit and matter are both part of existence, are in harmony with each other, we shall realise that it is wrong to feel that it is somehow shameful or non-spiritual to desire material things.

Yet, this is what we are often led to believe. Certainly there is nothing wrong with an attitude of making do with the minimum, in leading a life of asceticism. Mahatma Gandhi led such a life but in his case as in yours it has to be a matter of choice. You follow such a lifestyle because it answers a need that arises from deep within you. However, making a virtue of sacrifice and what is forced upon you—to celebrate suffering—is a different thing altogether. This was the basis of my decision to contact our young. To know their dreams and tell them that it is perfectly all right to dream of a good life, an abundant life, a life full of pleasures and comforts, and work for that golden era. Whatever you do must come from the heart, express your spirit, and thereby you will also spread love and joy around you.

My first such meeting took place in a high school in Tripura. It was a gathering of 500 students and teachers. After my talk on the second vision for transforming India into a developed nation, there were a series of questions, two of which I would like to discuss. The first question was: 'Where do we get a role model from, how do you get a role model?'

Whether we are aware of it or not, from childhood onwards, through various phases of life, we adopt role models. I said, 'When you are growing up, say till the age of fifteen, the best role model I can think of would be your father, your mother and your schoolteacher.' They, to my mind, are the people who can impart the best guidance during this period. I turned to the teachers and parents present there and told them what a big responsibility they have. I personally believe the full development of a child with a value system can only come from these people. In my own home, when I was growing up, I used to see my father and mother say namaz five times a day, and in spite of their modest financial resources, I found them always giving to the needy around. My teacher, Sivasubramania Iyer, was responsible for persuading my father to send me to school setting aside financial constraints. It is very important for every parent to be willing to make the. effort to guide children to be good human beings—enlightened and hard-working. The teacher, the child's window to learning and knowledge, has to play the role model in generating creativity in the child. This triangle is indeed the real role model I can think of. I would even go to the extent of saying that if parents and teachers show the required dedication to shape the lives of the young, India would get a new life. As it is said: Behind the parents stands the school, and behind the teacher the home. Education and the teacher-student relationship have to be seen not in business terms but with the nation's growth in mind. A proper education would help nurture a sense of dignity and self-respect among our youth. These are qualities no law can enforce—they have to be nurtured ourselves.

The children enjoyed this answer though I don't know whether the parents and teachers got the message.

Another girl in all seriousness asked, 'Every day we read in the newspaper or hear our parents talk about atankvadies (terrorists). Who are they? Do they belong to our country?' This question really shocked me. I myself was searching for an answer. They are our own people. Sometimes we create them through political and economic isolation. Or they can be fanatics, sometimes sponsored by hostile nations, trying to disrupt normal life through terrorism. I looked at the audience, at the people sitting by my side, at the teachers, and at the sky for an answer. I said, 'Children, I am reminded of our epics, the Ramayana and the Mahabharata. In the Ramayana the battle is between the divine hero Rama and the demon king Ravana. It is a long-drawn battle that finally Rama wins. In the Mahabharata, there is the battle at Kurukshetra. In this fight between good and evil, Dharma wins again. The battles are many but finally peace triumphs. In our times too we have seen this battle between good and evil—for instance, the Second World War. It seems to me that both good and evil will survive side by side. The Almighty does help them both to various degrees! How to minimize the evil through our spiritual growth is a question that has persisted throughout human history.'

On another occasion, I addressed a very large gathering of students at St Mary's School, Dindigul in Tamil Nadu on their seventy-fifth anniversary celebrations. Among the large number of children wishing to meet me were two who were in a hurry to get an answer from me. One student asked, 'I have read your book *Agni Siragugal* (the Tamil version of *Wings of Fire*). You always give a message to dream. Tell me, why dream?'

My answer was to ask the gathered children to recite the following: 'Dream, dream, dream. Dream transforms into thoughts. Thoughts result in actions.' I told them, 'Friends, if there are no dreams, there are no revolutionary thoughts; if there are no thoughts, no actions will emanate. Hence, parents and teachers should allow their children to dream. Success always follows dreams attempted though there may be some setbacks and delays.'

Another boy asked, 'Please tell me, who would be the first scientist in the world?' It occurred to me— science was born and survives only by questions. The whole foundation of science is questioning. And as parents and teachers well know, children are the source of unending questions. Hence, 'Child is the first scientist,' I replied. There was thunderous applause. The children enjoyed this different way of thinking. Teachers and parents also smiled at the answer.

During my visit to Assam, I visited Tezpur. I had gone for the convocation ceremony of Tezpur University and also to receive the honorary doctorate conferred on me. After the convocation, I took off to meet schoolchildren. It was a big gathering of young people. The theme of my address was 'Indomitable Spirit'. As soon as I finished my talk the youngsters mobbed me for autographs. When I finished giving autographs I faced two interesting questions. One was: 'Why cannot water from the Brahmaputra, which is in flood much of the time, be diverted to Rajasthan or Tamil Nadu which are starved of water?'

Only children will have these innovative ideas. Grown-ups tend to see more impossibilities. It was such a powerful question, I was completely beaten. I was sure even the Prime Minister would not have been able to answer it! How to tell the boy, rivers are a state subject and our states are fighting for the rights to their waters? That these would bring them prosperity some day but meanwhile they were flowing wastefully into the sea and causing floods every year. How to answer it?

I said, 'India Vision 2020 demands from the young that they start a great mission of connecting rivers cutting across the states.' I personally feel the young have the most powerful minds. They can overcome the negativity of the bureaucracy and some self-centred policies of the state governments to enrich the people of the country. They can even improve

coordination between the states and the Centre. And they surely will!

Another student asked me a question for which again I had no ready answer. He said, 'Sir, big leaders in any field don't come and talk to us. We see our Prime Minister often going to Chennai, Lucknow, and many places. But he never comes here. We want him; we want to talk to him.' I was impressed by this urge to communicate with the country's leaders. I said, when I reach Delhi, I will tell your dream to the leaders and your dream will come true.

I later narrated this to the Prime Minister. He conceded the point and said, 'Children don't talk to me any more. Maybe the security cordon has created a separation.' I request our leaders in different fields to interact more with the children of the country for a better understanding of their own purpose in life as also for helping create a better future for our children. I have visited Jharkhand a number of times after its formation. Every time I visit it, I am struck by the tremendous resources that wait to be harnessed in the state, which will multiply its wealth manifold. At the Sri Ramakrishna High School, Bokaro, I addressed a gathering of about 3,000 students and saw their creativity on display in an exhibition of their paintings, toys and other items made by them. In my conversation with them, one student asked me, 'In Jharkhand, it is green everywhere. We have forests, streams and hills. Why is it that we have a desert in Rajasthan?'

The question reminded me of a similar one in Assam: Why cannot the Brahmaputra's waters be taken to Tamil Nadu and Rajasthan? 'You know, twenty years ago, you would not have seen much cultivation in Rajasthan. But once the Indira Gandhi Canal was constructed agriculture became possible in many places. It is possible for man to transform the desert into a fertile land.' I repeated what I had told the student in Assam. 'It has to be one of the greatest missions of India to connect rivers so that water can reach many water-starved states. Visionary action is needed. When you grow up you will probably be part of reconstructing this nation and giving shape to these thoughts.'

One child came to me with a serious expression and asked, 'Sir, will your Agni missile cross the ocean and reach America?'

I was a little startled by this thought. 'For us no country is our enemy to send Agni there. Particularly America is our friend. Agni symbolises our strength. It shows that India has all the capabilities.'

During my visit to Cuttack I participated in the birthday celebrations of the late Justice Harihar Mahapatra. I went there at the invitation of Justice Ranganath Mishra. For me, it was a revelation, how the independence movement, the first vision for the nation, had created the larger-than-life figure of Justice Harihar Mahapatra. He lived to the age of ninety-two and established Cuttack Eye Hospital, Utkal University and above all organised multi-pronged efforts to remove poverty. My biography in Oriya was released. At the end of my speech the youngsters crowding around put forth many questions.

The first question was, 'Sir, tell us which are your favourite books, that you loved and which have shaped your mind?'

I said, 'Four books in my life have been very close to my heart. I cherish reading them. The first is *Man the Unknown* by Dr. Alexis Carrel, a doctor-turned-philosopher and a Nobel laureate. This book highlights how the mind and body both have to be treated in an ailment as the two are integrated. You cannot treat one and ignore the other. In particular, children who dream of becoming doctors should read the book. They will learn that the human body is not a mechanical system;

it is a very intelligent organism with a most intricate and sensitive feedback system. The second book, one I venerate, is Tiruvalluvar's *Thirukkural,* which provides an excellent code of life. The third is *Light from Many Lamps* by Lillian Eichler Watson which has touched me deeply. It illuminates how we live and has been an invaluable guide to me for fifty years. And the Holy Quran is, of course, a constant companion.'

While I was addressing another gathering of school children in Anand, Gujarat, one smart boy asked a very intelligent question: 'Who is our enemy?' I liked the question and put it to the other students, encouraging them to come forward with their views. Then came the answer, 'Poverty'. What a wise reaction from this young child whom I have mentioned in the dedication.

The last question, which I am including here, came from the powerful mind of another child. 'Tell me, sir, are Pakistani weapons stronger than Indian ones?' I asked the child why this doubt arose in his mind. Reports he read in the media led him to think so, he said.

'This is a unique characteristic of our country— to belittle our capabilities. It may even be genetic!' I said. 'India can design, develop and produce any type of missile and any type of nuclear weapon. This is a capability only four countries in the world have. You remove all the doubts from your mind,' I told the child, who gave me a very satisfied look.

I have selected only eleven questions here from among the hundreds of questions I have been asked during the course of meeting 40,000 high school students so far. The questions reflect the children innocence, but most of all they show how strongly they feel the desire to live in a strong and prosperous nation. I also realised from these sessions how important it is for them to have role models, whether in science, industry, sports, entertainment or some other field. The question is: Can we give our children a role model? And how?

At the dawn of the new millennium came the news that the human genome had been decoded. All the 30, 000 genes that human beings carry today, we are told, are identical to those of our Stone Age ancestors who lived thousands of years ago. One of the traits that has come down to us from them, along with others that are needed for survival, is the desire for achievement.

It is said that nature gave us this instinct because the need to achieve, like the need to reproduce, the need to eat, the need to drink and the need to breathe, is simply too important to be left to chance. History shows the hunger for achievement is a highly evolved one and undoubtedly the strongest one. We tend to forget it but it underlines much of our experience. Most important, without it, how would we learn and grow, aspire to greater perfection?

I have seen Dr. Vikram Sarabhai's vision succeeding over three decades through sustained and coordinated achievement. At work in that and any other endeavour was this same desire to exceed the limits. As we try and excel, role models play a guiding role. The power of Vikram Sarabhai was such that others took up his vision and completed it long after he was no more. For you it could be someone else whom you admire—a sportsperson, a teacher, a successful entrepreneur.

I recently had the chance to meet a legendary personality, a role model herself. Lata Mangeshkar was presiding over a function in remembrance of her father, Master Deenanath Mangeshkar. Lata Mangeshkar is a recipient of the Bharat Ratna and I felt honoured that she had asked me to inaugurate the 450-bed Deenanath Hospital and Research Centre in Pune. I visited the hospital just before the inauguration. I found that it would be treating nearly 30 per cent of the patients free. I was touched by the fact that despite her wealth and fame, she had not lost sight of the fact that one needs to do all one can to help relieve the suffering of others.

Her songs played over the radio have brought pleasure to countless hearts over the decades. During the India-China conflict in 1962, her song *'Ae mere vatan ke logo'* moved an entire nation. Few people can claim to have influenced the lives of millions in such a delightful way.

Role models can help us focus on what is correct for us as individuals, as groups and, of course, as a nation. They can also lead us to great success. We seem to have got carried away with the success of a few in the field of information technology. But that is indeed nothing compared to what we can and should achieve. Ancient India was a knowledge society and a leader in many intellectual pursuits, particularly in the fields of mathematics, medicine and astronomy. A renaissance is imperative for us to once again become a knowledge superpower rather than simply providing cheap labour in areas of high technology.

Summary

A nation's wealth is the young generation of the country. When they grow up, who can be the role models? Mother, father and elementary school teachers play a very important part as role models. When the child grows up, the role models will be national leaders of quality and integrity in every field including politics, the sciences, technology and industry.

□

Letter to His Son's Teacher

—Abraham Lincon

He will have to learn, I know,
that all men are not just,
all men are not true.
But teach him also that
for every scoundrel there is a hero;
that for every selfish Politician,
there is a dedicated leader...
Teach him for every enemy there is
a friend,

Steer him away from envy,
if you can,
teach him the secret of
quiet laughter.

Let him learn early that
the bullies are the easiest to lick...
Teach him, if you can,
the wonder of books...
But also give him quiet time
to ponder the eternal mystery of birds
in the sky,
bees in the sun,

and the flowers on a green hillside.
In the school teach him
it is far honourable to fail
than to cheat...
Teach him to have faith
in his own ideas,
even if everyone tells him
they are wrong...
Teach him to be gentle
with gentle people,
and tough with the tough.

Try to give my son
the strength not to follow the crowd
when everyone is getting on the band wagon
Teach him to listen to all men...
but teach him also to filter
all he hears on a screen of truth,
and take only the good
that comes through.

Teach him if you can,
how to laugh when he is sad...
Teach him there is no shame in tears,
Teach him to scoff at cynics
and to beware of too much sweetness...
Teach him to sell his brawn
and brain to the highest bidders
but never to put a price-tag
on his heart and soul.

Teach him to close his ears
to a howling mob
and to stand and fight
if he thinks he's right.

Treat him gently,
but do not cuddle him,
because only the test
of fire makes fine steel.

Let him have the courage
to be impatient...
let him have the patience to be brave.
Teach him always
to have sublime faith in himself,
because then he will have
sublime faith in mankind.

This is a big order,
but see what you can do...
He is such a fine fellow,
my son!

(Abraham Lincoln)

Every Child is Special

—Aamir Khan

Aamir Khan who is known as 'Mister Perfectionist' has given excellent films such as 'Lagan', 'Gazani', 'Mangal Pandey', 'Three Idiots' and 'Tare Jamin Par'. For his contribution in the field of art he has been awarded with Padmashree and Padma Bhushan.

During a programme of teachers and parents he told that for him joy of children is the most important. Excerpts of his talk are: "Every child has got one or other quality. We will have to identify that quality. We can not pressurize every child to come first in his class. Liking of the child be appreciated and he be inspired for becoming a good human being. Teachers should concentrate on any child who is poor in studies. "

Films on Education

I am not from the field of Education. I am an Actor. During last few years I got some experience about Education. I did

two films namely 'Tare Jamin Par' and 'Three Idiots' which were related to Education. For doing these films I did a lot of studies and have tried to know the facts related to the education system of the Country. Here today many teachers, mother-fathers and children are present. I want to put forward view regarding Education. I am not aware that upto what level you will agree to it, but I have my own views about education which I will put forward.

Identify Good Things

First of all I would like to say that every child is special, this I have gathered from my research. Every child has got one or the other quality. Being Parents it is our responsibility to identify that quality and to help in improving that. Every one of us have got strength and weaknesses. I have also got strength and weaknesses. We will have to see likings and dislikings of a child. We will have to understand his likings. Child may have weaknesses as well. We will have to help him so that he can come out of that weakness.

Child's Laughter

Many a time school authorities proudly intimate me that all the children of the School are passed. Our results are cent percent. I only have a question to them—how many children are happy? Studies are alright but how many children are happy. For me their happiness, laughs are of more value. Is the child perturbed with the load of studies or you are putting undue pressure on him? I have seen that even in Lower KG class pressure is placed on the child for attaining first position. Every mother-father wish that their child should come first in Nimbu-Chamcha race. Yes, the same rate in which children run after keeping lemon and spoon in their mouth. Children ought to be given a natural environment.

Unnecessary Race

Our education system is such that from the beginning we put pressure on the child to stand first in the class. This has happened with me also. We ask the child when he comes back from school-what position did you get in the class? If he says 'Second' he is scolded. If his rank is 9th or 10th, he is in trouble. How can every child stand FIRST and what sort of race are we imposing on him? Be mindful where will the child lead through this pressure? What impact his heart and mind will have through this race for becoming first. These questions are to be considered. I wish that the people connected with Education must think over this.

Bad Interest will Increase

When we exert pressure on a child to remain at number One, a thinking comes in his mind to defeat all by whatever means. He thinks that becoming first is the only aim of his life.

Many a time the spirit of remaining ahead of everybody makes him selfish and so he thinks about himself only. I say that when a child comes back from school we should ask 'to whom have you helped today and because of you who smiled? We should inculcate a desire in him to help others. If we give such motivation to the child his view point about life will change, and when these children will grow, the Society will change. Then our Society will have such younger generation which will have concern and care for Society-then only we will be able to create a better Society.

Pious Person: Gentleman

Instead of improving unnecessary competition in children we should make them a good human being. My desire is that the education system should be such that enables grown ups to lead a respectable life. They should have a feeling to help others. They should become responsible citizens —not thinking only about themselves but for the entire Society. There should not be liking only to earn money. Along with themselves the concern for Society is also important.

Degree is not the Meaning of Education

Education does not mean obtaining of degree. I feel that Education is beyond Degrees and Marks obtained. Education does not mean copycat of books. Education is that knowledge which gives us courage to ask questions, to face challenges and to invent new things. I act in films. People say that I am a good actor but I wish to tell you that I don't have any Certificate for acting. Yes, I love acting, it is my passion, my love and my strength too. Therefore instead of running for a degree we should do what we like.

□

Peace will Establish through Education

—Shakira

Izabel Mebarak Ripol Shakira is a singer, dancer as well as a Choreographer. With her music album "Hips don't Lie" Shakira got laurel world over. She is from Columbia. She is keenly interested in social work. Through her Foundation she is doing work on a large scale for children Education. Produced here below are extracts of her talk at Oxford University.

Poor children should get free education. Free education does not mean Charity. Spending on children education means investment for an improved future. By sending them to school you can stop them from going for terrorism, drugs and crime.

I must confess, I am somewhat mystified as to why you are here. I won't be singing... and there won't be any hip shaking.

So, how do I, a girl from Barranquilla, Colombia come to occupy the same stage as Newton and Churchill? Lord knows I'm no Mother Teresa, but here I am, nonetheless.

I realise that the one point of view from which I can depart is that of an artist. After all, it is who I am. We artists depend on our imaginations.

When I first learned I was coming, I thought about the past and I imagined the future. From your minds, ideas will sprout that will give new shape to the world. I cannot help but fast-forward to what the world will be like in 50 years. What will be happening? Who will we be? How will we live? What challenges can we overcome?

I have a fantasy about this future that I want to share with you.

Let me put it this way, if civilisation were a car, we would have been cruising at 20 miles per hour for millions of years only to hit light speed in the last hundred.

What made us accelerate so quickly recently and how can we continue this pace? There is only one explanation: the democratization of education...

It is the airplane that brought me to England, the medicine that allows grandparents to meet their grand children, the philosophy that expands our individual liberties, and the technology that sent us to the moon.

I do not subscribe to the idea that the older days were better days. I strongly believe that the best is yet to come...

Like John Locke, I am too impatient to wait. He says it, I sing it: "Why wait for later; I'm not a waiter. " I like to make things happen, (by the way, that's from a song on my new album "She Wolf" in stores now). Anyways...

I know that education is our ticket.

How do I know? Because I've seen it.

I was born and raised in a country marked by civil conflict, social strife and inequality. Growing up in the developing world, where education is perceived as a luxury and not as right; where children beg for an education and parents are desperate to provide it; where if one is born poor, one is destined to do die poor...

I'm still a student on all these issues, but I've come to learn that there are ways to change this. So no government can say that the challenge of bringing education to every child is an impossible task. Because we know how to enroll all those 75 million kids who don't have access to any kind of primary education, by:

Abolishing school fees.

Hiring quality teachers.

Providing uniforms and textbooks to children.

And providing most importantly food, because no kid can learn on an empty stomach and because we've proven that it becomes the best incentive for parents to send their kids to school and reduce child labor.

Now I want to be clear about this, this isn't about charity. This is about investing in human potential...

So I look to you to help us go faster. I look to you to foster—no, more than that, to become—the network of collaborative minds that can stimulate the evolution of human understanding...

That is how I want the youth of 2060 to see us. That our mission for global peace consisted of sending 30, 000 educators to Afghanistan, not 30, 000 soldiers. That in 2010, world education became more important than world domination.

Because only education will accelerate our evolution.

Only by investing in our children, by tapping their potential that has remained untapped for too long, can they one day cure our diseases, or bring us to Mars, or secure us peace here on earth.

Because, it bears repeating, we are one world.

One civilisation.

One conscience.

One engine.

One destiny.

And so, if I have just one more thought to offer you and to add to our one collective conscience here today, it is this:

Education for all.

John Locke, who I believe was one of yours, once said, "the only fence against the world is a thorough knowledge of it, and the earlier the better. " So yeah, the earlier the better. There is no time to waste. It is you who are in the driver's seat. It is your foot on the accelerator.

And please, step on it.

□

Child

—Binodanand Jha

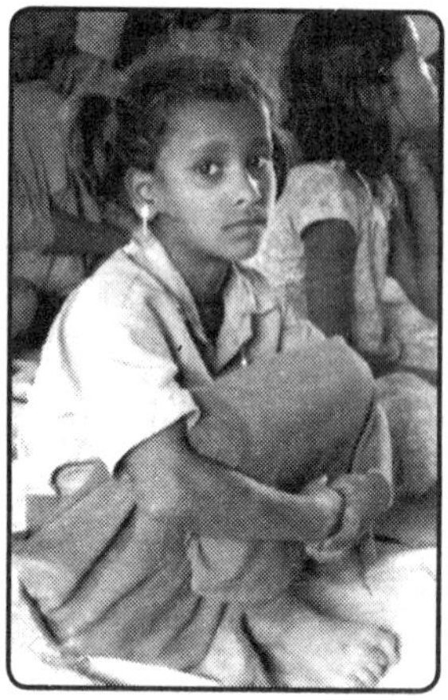

Has saying by a Child ever surprised you? Off and On Mothers discuss what their Soni (name of the child) has told today. Many a time you may have noticed that your son has done something good and that you narrate to your family members and friends. This happens quite often but because of various prejudices we underestimate our children who are more capable than what we think of. That is why we are unable to understand them. A child having immense inquisitiveness has come to this world with visualisation, creativity and a great capacity to learn.

You can see the creative spark and if you don't make any interference; you will be surprised to see the small children's personal intrinsic abilities or nature and the activities done through that. You will also be surprised to find some secret behind every activity and this has to be understood. Children touch, break and assemble the things. They grasp things related to environment quickly. Merely at the age of three they talk supportive grammatical concepts. We will have to understand their mental status, psychology and aspirations—

then only we can promote their mental strength.

We can not compare a child with a doll. However just for the sake of understanding we may take him like a plant. Within him all the qualities and tendencies required for inner development are available and only things required are the fertiliser, water and security. Output placed is more than the input taken by a child. Many a time children ask such questions for which we do not have answers, but those questions are reasoned and also can not be contradicted.

Intrinsic Qualities

It is necessary to understand intrinsic qualities of a child; this can help us developing the child in class room. Such intrinsic qualities are` discussed here.

Inquisitiveness

Children by nature are inquisitive. In their surroundings they find thousands of things scattered. This makes them keen to know, ask many questions and remain eager to know their answers. It is necessary to increase their 'to know' desire. In case they are not satisfied with any answer they themselves make efforts to find the answer. Is 'to know' desire in a child not to be promoted?

Activeness

Few children because of their 'to know' desire also do 'mischief' but this mischief is not aimed toward making any loss to anybody, rather it is for satisfying their own inquisitiveness, which we may call 'Over-activeness'. Children always want to do something, either by assembling or dismantling. By this process they want to reach to a conclusion and also to observe what happens with this. Therefore by using their activeness in the right way abilities be improved so that their thoughts and creativity are enlightened. Mostly it has been observed that those children who are playful in the beginning become creative to the same extent when they grow up.

Likings

Children by nature are playful. Their attention does not remain on one thing for long. They blissfully seek change and so their attention usually gets distracted. Such distraction happens when they consider another condition more joyful than the present one and also think they can contribute more in another condition.

Restrictions on their activeness are disliked by the children. They prefer freedom. By restrictions they lose interest on all things. So to keep their interest intact they be allowed to work freely. In such a way they require full freedom for thinking. For this reason the importance should also be given to freedom required for the process of learning.

This freedom must have discipline also but the type of discipline should be such that they themselves are encouraged to obey that. They should not feel that unnecessary restrictions are imposed. Generally children themselves are keen on discipline by nature, but they do not like imposition of discipline. They remain disciplined in any game or work which they like. They remain attentive and concentrated where the work is of their liking.

Creativity

Children have got creativity. Imagination is the basis of their creativity. They have enormous capacity for creating things. Therefore, from the scattered things in their environment they make creative contributions. In accordance to their mind they prepare one or other thing, we may not feel it appropriate(probably we are not in a position to understand and appreciate their creation) but a sign of satisfaction is there on their face when they complete the work. They have a feeling of satisfaction– that this creative work has been done by them.

Children through their imagination make new inventions, may be we do not give due respect to it. Children expect respect from elders for their creation—now tell how would you develop creative quality in children—a serious thought needed for that.

Working in a Group

Children like to work in the group of same age and friends. By this they can share their feelings, efforts and experiences with one another. In fact in the same age group it is easy to express feelings and views whereas they feel cut off from elder group due to difference in behaviour. This facility they find among their own age group—there they can express without any hesitation.

Children's Personal Thinking and Angle of Seeing

Children have their own thinking. They see the things as per their perception, take a view on that and then remain firm on that generally. However they change that with the passage of time or make amends. To know their angle we will have to see that as per their level. Instead of ignoring them we should form view as per their level. Whether the angle of children is different than that of elders. If yes, how?

Capacity to Recognise

Children have got capacity to understand grief-happiness, right and wrong. From their angle they try to make distinct identity in every field. Children through logic design the things. They only want a helper, who can promote their views as well as thinking. It is necessary that they should get opportunity for thoughts as well as anxieties and solution to them. For this the children shall be given opportunity for discussion. In case the flow of their views is stopped somewhere they are to be taken back to the earlier stream. It is very necessary to practice this in Class room.

Absorbing Capacity of the Children

Every child has got different capacity for absorption. Some children can learn many things at a time but some can learn one at a time. Children learn something or the other from all the activities of life. They also learn from the mistakes they commit.

Many a time when we feel that the children are following in fact they decide on the results as to what has to be done in future, but their absorbing capacity depends on their interest and inclination. For us the question is where and by which method we can create interest in them for all round development.

John Halt, the writer of 'Why Children Fail', focusing on his teaching experience has explained that we adults many a time do not act humble and natural with children. Before them we pose ourselves as if we are the knowledgeable and almighty. We should have relation of love and happiness with the Children. Children have pleasure in asking questions. So those questions which we can not reply immediately, our answer should be that at present I will not be able to answer.

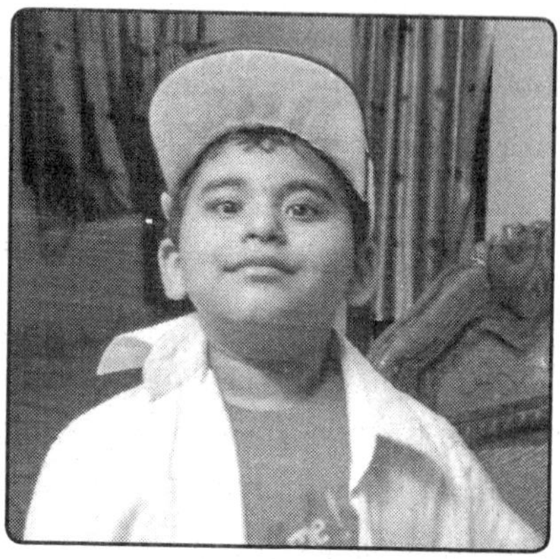

In this way while working with the children we should not impose our knowledge on them, but try to understand their psychology. Before them we need to present ourselves in such a manner that they can express without any hesitation. They are to be helped keeping in view their problems and questions, then only we will be able to provide them appropriate assistance. This is difficult but not so much that we cannot do.

□

'Padho Purbi Champaran' Special Programme for Improving Basic Reading

—Rukmini Banerjee

Introduction

Bihar, like India, has made impressive strides in ensuring schooling access to children and in reaching close to universal enrollment. Now that almost all children in the age group 6 to14 are enrolled in school, the focus is shifting to what happens inside the school. Increasingly for the last decade or so, the issue of children learning is beginning to occupy a central position in discussions of educational policy and practice. Whether it is student achievement surveys by NCERT or household assessments of basic learning done by ASER, all available data point to the fact that children are far behind as compared to where they are expected to be as per curriculum standards.

Due to a variety of related reasons, many children do not make adequate progress in school and begin to fall behind academically. A vast majority of children, especially in rural communities do not get much learning support at home. In school, teaching activities are based on the textbook for the grade and children are expected to learn at the pace of the textbook. If the child cannot keep up, then she or he begins to fall behind. This lag in learning is cumulative. As a result, in every grade/standard, there are children with different levels of ability to read, write and do arithmetic. For example, it is not uncommon in a Std. 5 class to find half of all children unable to do what is expected of them in Std. 2.

This huge range and diversity in learning levels makes it difficult for a teacher to teach the textbook or curriculum expected of that class. Despite working hard, the teacher is often frustrated and disheartened because children are not making progress. Despite attending school, many children get demotivated because they feel they are not able to keep up with what is expected of them. Parents who are watching from afar can see that their children are not learning adequately and so become disappointed with the school. Naturally the situation worsens if children do not attend or if teachers do not teach. The lack of learning brings the situation to what is often called a 'big stuck'.

To get the education system moving forward again, it is important to be able to get out of the 'big stuck'. Children who have 'fallen behind' need focused help to enable them to start from where they are to catch up. It is only when this is done that children can have a real opportunity to complete primary schooling and achieve a satisfactory level of learning. The first step in this process is to ensure their basic skills are strengthened. Without being able to read, children cannot progress further in education or in life.

Key Elements of Padho Purbi Champaran Model

Given the realities on the ground, the district education administration in East Champaran headed by Dr. Binodanand Jha (DEO) decided to try a large scale model of accelerated reading. The decision was to implement this programme on scale to see what kind of outcomes would result focused approach that used existing resources but reorganised teaching-learning activities within school day. The district education administration approached Pratham – a well known NGO who has done similar activities elsewhere in Bihar and in India to help with this approach. The district administration and Pratham together developed a 'special teaching-learning' package for children currently in Std3, 4 and 5. The initiative was called 'Padho Purbi Champaran'. The entire effort was organised around the five core principles:

Children who have 'fallen behind' need immediate and focused help to build basic skills like reading.

Learning goals need to be clearly articulated and understood. In Purbi Champaran, the goal was to ensure that every child in Std. 3, 4 and 5 would be able to read Std. 2 level text fluently in four months. This goal was widely publicised to parents and community members.

Assessment was an integral part of the effort. A simple assessment was done at the start of the programme for every child to ensure that every teacher was aware of the current reading level of each and every child. Teachers periodically assessed children to gauge progress. The most effective way to help these children, especially those in Std. 3, 4 and 5 is to group children by their reading level rather than by grade and teach them using appropriate activities and materials.

The most sustainable way to improve children learning is to ensure that these efforts are led by people from within the system like the Cluster Resource Centre Coordinators who can guide, mentor, demonstrate, monitor and support each school in their charge. The special learning package was also conducted within school hours.

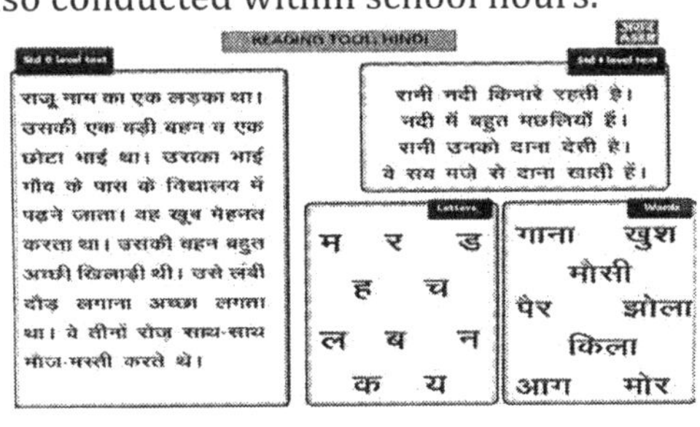

Preparatory Phase

Selection of blocks: Five blocks were chosen to participate in this programme. These were Patahi, Dhaka, Ghorasahan, Sugauli and Harsiddhi. Several of these are educationally backward blocks of the district.

Orientation and training of CRCCs: In the last week of August, all CRCCs of five blocks participated in a three day training organised by Pratham. In all there were 45 CRCCs and 5 Block resource persons. In an interesting exercise, the CRCCs were asked to estimate enrolment, attendance and learning level of children in Std. 3 to 5. After putting down their estimates, they were divided into groups of three and sent to 5 schools. To their surprise, although their estimates of children attendance were close to what they found in schools, their estimates of learning levels were way off the mark (i. e., much lower). This was an eye-opener for CRCCs.

Simple task made the rationale for the programme very evident to the participants. The training was in an interactive and hands-on way. The first day was spent in understanding the rationale of basic reading assessment. The tool and the information from the assessment was used in two ways – the first was to group children by their level of reading rather than by grade and the second was to track the progress of the children till they reached their goal – being able to fluently read and understand a simple story (at least at Std. 2 level).

Training of cluster coordinators focused on using the assessment tool to create groups ('mahal') of children by their reading level and then practicing activities suited for each level. All of this was practiced in nearby schools. The participants and trainers would go to nearby schools so that they could watch demonstrations by trainers and also practice activities under the watchful eye of the trainers.

Practice classes by CRCCs: In the next step of the process, it was decided that each CRCC would conduct a practice class with the same children for 15 days continuously. This would enable the CRCC to actually carry out what he or she would guide the teachers to do later. In order to provide academic leadership, it is essential that the cadre that leads has actually been able to deliver the outcomes that they will expect teachers to deliver. Two or three CRCCs worked together in a school during the practice class phase. Each had a group of children by level that they worked with. The 'practice' classes were immensely effective in helping CRCCs to understand the challenges and intricacies of teaching and learning in an actual school environment. It also helped them to have a first-hand experience of how much progress children can make when the entire system (training, assessment, teaching-learning, materials) is geared to achieving a basic goal.

The 'practice' class data shows how quickly children can make progress if the entire effort is geared to helping them to achieve the learning goals that have been set. If children who can read paragraphs and stories are considered to be 'readers', then we can see that in the baseline about 24% children were 'readers'. 15 days of instruction later, the same figure has risen to almost 45%. The experience from the 'practice' classes also indicated that learning by doing is one of the most effective ways of making people capable of implementing a new approach.

Practice classes data : CRCCs in E. Champaran September 2012

Std. 3-5 Reading levels	*Baseline*		*Endline after 15 days*	
	Children	%	*Children*	%
Story	22	2. 3	215	22. 2
Paragraph	205	21. 5	216	22. 2
Word	206	21. 6	261	27
Letter	314	32. 8	198	20. 5
Beginner	208	21. 8	78	8. 1
Total	955	100	968	100

Even in the 15 days, clear improvements were visible. The enthusiasm of the CRCCs was also palpable. Schools, teachers and CRCCs realised the effective and engaging instruction to make progress and the power to energise the whole system and bring about significant changes in a period of time.

Activity package and appropriate materials: To learn to read, children must have material to read that is at their own level. Each child in the programme was given a booklet of simple stories and also a barahkhadi chart. This was the only additional cost in the programme provided by SSA. For each group of children, the teacher/instructor carried out a set of different activities on a daily basis. The basic activities included the following:

Reading a story aloud and discussion: This was done to provide 'role model' for reading and to develop children's ability to discuss what has been read. The story booklet was essential for this because as the story was being read out aloud either by the teacher or other students, every student could follow it in their own copy of the book. The discussion about the story helped to build understanding and comprehension and developed the text-transaction capability in children.

Activities with the barahkhadi chart: The traditional barahkhadi chart provides an excellent opportunity to develop the sight-sound connections for children who are learning to read. A variety of different activities are done with the barahkhadi chart – including, reading it aloud with clear pronunciation. Children could read aloud horizontally, vertically and also randomly from the middle. Other games can also be played with the barahkhadi chart. The drills done with this chart reinforce recognition of the consonant-vowel unit and the consequent patterns - an essential component of learning to read.

Word games: Depending on the level of the group, different kinds of word games are played to improve vocabulary, phonemic awareness and automaticity.

Writing: Research and experience with young children indicate that writing activities also help children to read. In addition, from the young age it is important to encourage children to express their own thoughts in their own words. Thus the writing time in this programme was an important one designed to develop Children's capabilities for expression.

Roll Out of the Program

There was an unforeseen delay in the roll out of the programme from the time of the CRCC classes. This was a delay of almost four months mainly due to delay in permissions and sanctions for printing of materials. In the last week of December 2012, training for teacher was organised in each cluster of the five selected blocks. Approximately 50 trainers from the government side and 45 trainers from Pratham worked together to conduct three day non-residential trainings for over 2300 teachers in 45 locations at the cluster level. The trainings followed the same pattern as that of CRCCs.

Monitoring and on-site support are key components for the success of any programme. In Padho Purbi Champaran, CRCCs and BRPs spent a lot of time in the field visiting schools, demonstrating activities and helping teachers and children.

Despite frequent breaks due to extreme cold, teachers' strike and other discontinuities, the programme ran from January till the end of April. End line assessment was conducted in May 2013.

Results

Altogether 681 schools were part of the pilot programme. More than 55, 000 children were included in the intervention. The table below shows the basic data for the five selected blocks.

No.	Name of Blocks	No. of Schools in each block	Enrollment in Std. 3, 4 and 5	Total children tested in pre test	Total children reached in programme (children below story level)	Total children tested in post level
1.	Dhaka	183	22767	19069	14348	13032
2.	Patahi	114	14858	9996	8265	7664
3.	Ghodasahan	98	15379	10564	8610	7618
4.	Sugauli	137	19599	14465	11892	11392
5.	Harsidhi	149	17859	15874	12424	11079
	Total	681	90462	69968	55539	50785

How much change in basic learning levels is possible in a four month period? Remember that the Padho Purbi Champaran classes were no more than an hour and a half each day. We estimate that only 60-70 days of instructional time was available to the schools to carry out this programme. At the start of the intervention there were no children who could read at Std. 2 level. By the end of this period, the proportion of children who could read stories had increased to 31%. If you add to that figure the proportion of children who could read at para level then the total proportion of 'readers' is over 50%.

PURBI CHAMPARAN DISTRICT : 681 schools. Std. 3-4-5. Jan-May 2013		
% Children at different reading levels		
Reading level	*Pre test %*	*Post-test%*
Story	0	31. 1
Para	22. 8	25. 5
Word	27. 1	24. 6
Letter	29. 7	14. 6

Beginner	20. 4	4. 2
Total %	100	100
Total tested	55539	50785

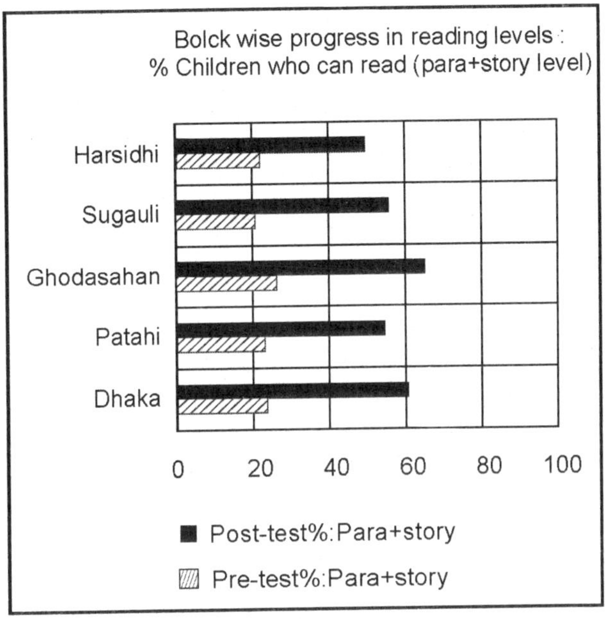

SOME CONCLUDING THOUGHTS

Achievements

- Daily attendance of children in school increased during this time. This was observed by the Pratham staff and the CRCCs.
- Improvements in reading were visible among children. The assessment data also reveals the improvements.
- In how the teachers and CRCCs spoke about children, it was clear that individual attention was being paid to the progress of children.

- Evidence of positive energy and enthusiasm among the CRCCs and teachers could be seen in most schools, a direct consequence of seeing students respond positively and quickly to their teaching.
- The strong leadership of the District Education officer and his commitment to the programme was a major influence on the work done by the team at district and block in education. The district and block teams which earlier had not implemented any serious learning improvement programme responded well to the disciplined and committed approach of their leader.

Obstacles and Constraints

The biggest obstacle for Padho Purbi Champaran was the delay in printing of materials and also the frequent holidays and discontinuities. Schools were closed or teaching did not happen almost every month for a variety of reasons like severe cold, teacher's strike etc.

Way Forward

Padho Purbi Champarn has served as a demonstration model for what is possible even with existing resources and within the existing government school system. From January 2013 onwards, discussions began at the state level about a possible statewide scale up. By April 2013, the state had decided that using experiences like that in East Champaran and a similar experience in Jehanabad, the entire state will take up basic reading improvement programmes. The 2013-2014 school year will show how much Bihar will learn from the Padho Purbi Champaran experience and how much will be put into practice. But what is certainly true is that a well-done experiment even in a few blocks in one district can go a long way in becoming a trendsetter for the future of children in the state.

□

Storytelling: What is the Use?

—Krishna Kumar

It is a great pity that our primary schools do not have a separate 'period' for storytelling for the first two grades each day. Such a provision would have solved at least a part of the problem we face in retaining children at school. Many will say that I am giving undue importance to this problem. I can well imagine many senior officers smiling cynically at my suggestion. Their vast experience and administrative wisdom have erased from their mind the knowledge I am sure they once possessed, that storytelling has a magical effect on children. It is terribly sad that even our teacher-training institutes do not take storytelling seriously, although some of them do remember to mention its importance during the course of training. I should like to imagine it is required to master at least thirty traditional stories. By 'master' I mean: to know the stories by hear, so one can tell them in a relaxed, confident manner. That is hardly a tall order for a society that has inherited thousands of stories from its past. Thirty stories that the teacher can tell at will can transform the ethos of the first two years of primary schooling, provided, of course, that the daily curriculum finds an honourable place for storytelling for its own sake.

In the preceding paragraph, I have used an adjective which I must explain before proceeding further. I have said

that I favour traditional stories. My experience of training young teachers in the art of storytelling is that when they are asked to look for stories to tell, they usually come up with stories published in a magazine for children or stories depicted as comics, and sometimes, even longish jokes and narratives of real events. Now, of course, all such material comes under the broad category called 'story' but not all such material can be expected to do the kind of magic we are hoping to perform with six- or seven-year-olds in a primary school. Stories that have come down to us from tradition have a special set of characteristics that contemporary stories presented in different forms and in the media do not necessarily possess. We shall soon see what these characteristics are, but let me first name a few sources of traditional stories. The *Panchatantra*, the *Jatakas*, the *Mahabharata*, the *Arabian Nights*, stories of Vikramaditya, and folktales from different regions come to mind as ready and rich sources. Then there are other selections like the *Kathasaritsagar*, the *Gulistan* and the *Bostan*, the Birbal stories and their counterparts, and folktales and fairytales from around the world. These resources are not easily accessible; so anyone who wants to introduce storytelling as a regular feature of the curriculum must ensure access to a selection of stories from these resources.

What Makes a Story Good for Telling?

If we want to know the characteristics of a good story, we cannot do better than to take a story children have enjoyed listening to for generations. The *Panchatantra* story of the lion and the rabbit is a fine example. The storyline is not as simple as one might assume on account of familiarity. Let us recall its main turning points. The day comes when the little rabbit must present himself before the old lion. By the time the rabbit shows up on the lion's doorstep, the lion is mad with hunger. In this critical moment, which is obviously unsuitable for any negotiation since the lion is so, so angry, the rabbit represents his case. How did he get so late? His story of meeting another lion on the way is, of course, totally untrue, but it evokes a response in the hungry and angry lion's royal mind. He now wants to settle his rival first, and so he goes with the rabbit to inspect the well where the rival lion supposedly lives. In this crucial moment, again, the rabbit depends on his ability to carry on with his bluff and on the mindless rage and jealousy he has aroused in the lion. On seeing his own image in the well, the lion cannot take it any more and jumps to his death.

Let us examine this old familiar story a little closely. For one thing, there is nothing trivial about its theme. Rather, it is about grave issues such as survival on the face of brute power and the threat of certain death. Normally, we keep such issues out of our conversation with children, but apparently, children have great interest in such issues. We may ask ourselves why, but I will come to that in a moment. Let me consider another important feature in the meantime. The story presents a small creature facing a crisis caused by a big, powerful creature. In order to survive the crisis, the small fellow uses a tactic which we normally consider immoral. During the course of applying this tactic, he displays some fine qualities of personality, such as courage and confidence in the face of danger, maintaining one's nerve right up to the end of a situation, and speaking to a powerful senior in socially approved ways. We must also notice the pace at which things move. The beginning establishes a strange kind of normalcy under which one animal is supposed to volunteer each day as food for the old king. Soon after this ominous routine is established, the little rabbit's turn comes, and the core of the story reveals itself. The rest of the incidents occur fast, for the rabbit cannot afford to lose a moment once he has taken the plunge into his dangerous strategy of survival. The listener is pushed from the situation to the next by means of dialogue, and it is quite clear that the listener of the story has no choice but to see everything from the rabbit's point of view.

This brief analysis should suffice to indicate some reasons for the immense popularity of this story with children. To begin with, it gives them a character or hero with whom they can fully identify. This character is the rabbit whose role in the story shares many of the predicaments and challenges that children face in their daily lives. He is small and powerless; he is required to do what he does not want to do; he is scared of dying at the hands of somebody who has total authority as well as physical force. These aspects of the rabbit's condition in the story have close parallels in every child's life, although we seldom notice them, busy as we are playing our roles as parents and teachers. Few of us know, for example, that sudden death is one of the biggest sources of anxiety in childhood; so is the prospect of being in a confrontation with someone big and strong.

The story draws children's attention as soon as it begins because children can see themselves in it. And then, what happens in it reinforces this attraction. The little rabbit chooses a strategy and it works. It not only works; it settles the problem forever, and for everyone. Now that is the kind of solution little children crave for. The strategy also has an attraction for them because it is based on the innocent desire they always carry which is to give an excuse. The rabbit's excuse for getting late has an extra element of fascination, or it is designed not just to save his own life, but also to kill the lion. Indeed, the rabbit's predicament is so dire precisely because he cannot save himself without destroying his oppressor. So, the story presents to its audience a great drama of survival by means of bravely carried out destruction. The only morality involved in it is the morality of self-survival. That too is something we cannot appreciate unless we perceive the story purely from the child's point of view. If we insist on seeing the story from an adult viewpoint, we are likely to conclude that it is an immoral story which, of course, it is.

What is the Use?

It should be clear by now that morality has nothing to

do with selecting a good story for children, at least in a direct sense. At a deeper level, the story of the rabbit and the lion has an inspiring element – it shows the advantages of staying cool while facing danger; it also shows how important it is to be thoughtful and imaginative. But these are hardly 'moral' lessons in a conventional sense. In fact, great traditional stories seldom teach conventional morality. More important for us is to recognise that moral development of the child is hardly the purpose of storytelling. The real gains of storytelling are quite different, and they can be listed as follows:

Storytelling promotes good listening: Who is a good listener? One who listens to the end. That is something we cannot say about many people. Even in formal discussions, people keep interrupting, partly because they are in the habit of assuming that they know in advance what the speaker is going to say, but often because they have no patience to listen. It is not surprising that listening is now regarded not merely as a skill but as an attitude, which high-level courses in management and administration find important to encourage. Storytelling promotes patient listening during the formative stage of our lives when the skill of listening and the attitude it implies towards the speaker have a good chance to become lifelong habits. It is somewhat strange that good listeners have become so rare in our country which has such an old and strong oral culture. My guess is that the neglect of storytelling during childhood has a lot to do with it. Modern India seems to have no time to tell stories regularly to children, and the consequences are becoming apparent.

Storytelling gives training in prediction: Children want to hear the stories they like again and again. The reason is that they use their familiarity with the story to test their own growing capacity to pay attention, but in an unconscious way. They enjoy the fact that during a second or third listening, they can successfully predict what will happen next. The joy of a prediction coming true is precisely what story-listening offers to an experienced listener; and it is not just joy; it reinforces the child-listener's confidence in his or her ability to predict. This confidence has a seminal role to play in all-round development, especially in learning how to read which is easily the biggest challenge of the first two years at school. But the ability to predict also has obvious uses in learning mathematics which works on the principle of rule-governed predictability of outcomes. Stories also have rules; it is just that these rules are of a metaphorical nature. For instance, many stories follow the rule that the small creature wins by tricking the big creature. This is what happens in the rabbit-and-lion story. As children hear more and more stories, they intuitively pick up the rules governing them, and the knowledge of these rules helps them become better predictors.

Stories extend our world: The world we carry in our heads or minds is what I am talking about. Stories extend it in the sense that they enable us to relate to things—both people and situations—that we never meet in our own lives. Why bother about such people or situations, then, one may ask—it is because they are part of life. Even if we do not meet them personally, they bother us in our thoughts, especially during childhood, but in a general sense, throughout our lifetime. Little children, for instance, worry about bad people even if none of the people surrounding them are particularly bad. Similarly, they secretly hope that they will get a chance to meet someone who is incredibly intelligent, beautiful, and good. The desire for ideal types as well as the fear of catastrophe is a part of the psychology of childhood. Traditional stories resonate this psychology, and, that is why, they attract children so readily. By listening to stories, the pre-literate child experiences by proxy a world much wider than his or her real world. Moreover, the experience that stories provide is not chaotic; rather it places a satisfying pattern or design on a chaotic world. That pattern is deeply 'moral', but not in a conventional sense. The victim does win, but often by using some objectionable means. The lie that the rabbit told the hungry lion is an example.

Stories give meaning to words: Finally, we can see the importance of storytelling in the manner that stories affect the child's expanding repertoire of language. Words are highly personal property, and the way words enable us to name the world is also highly personal. Yet, words are also a social wealth in as much as we use words to share our experiences with others. Meanings attach to words on account of this double-faced quality of words. For example, the child knows from personal experience what it is to feel hungry, but that personal meaning also helps him to appreciate how the lion in the story must have felt when he was hungry. The story enables the listener to slightly stretch the meaning of the word 'hungry' so as to include the lion in it. The more stories one listens to, the more one's vocabulary becomes capable of including in its orbit of meaning the experiences that others bring to us. Seen this way, stories told during childhood become precursors of reading.

Indeed, all the four points discussed above in the context of storytelling are applicable to reading as well. Children ability to read bring into play their familiarity with the rules and structures of a language. Competence in reading is crucially dependent on the ability to predict or to make an intelligent guess. On the basis of their familiarity with the structures of a language, children try to guess what might come next in a sentence or narration. Seen this way, storytelling is highly relevant to the development of literacy skills.

Beyond Use

Telling stories on a regular basis can help it achieve these goals But, it does little justice to the heritage of storytelling to place it in this kind of instrumentalist frame of appreciation, even if our primary concern is to promote it in the present-day school system. The alternative is to appreciate storytelling for its intrinsic worth which lies in its pluralistic inheritance. Storytelling deserves to be seen as a civilisational practice which permits us to protect the diversity of cultural experiences and stances from the homogenising effects of modem education and media. Storytelling also needs to be celebrated as an oral heritage, in the obvious sense that its aesthetic merits and appeal evolved by means of oral communication and memory, as well as with reference to the oral competence that storytelling as an everyday practice calls for. It is in this wider frame of worth that we ought to identify its significance and role for young children at school.

We can distinguish storytelling as an aspect of the human heritage from the skill or craft involved in the act of telling a story. As a heritage, it forms the centre of practices which enabled extended communities to symbolically represent their distinct insights and wisdom. Stories told over time in distinct geographical regions and cultures became characteristic of those cultures. Centuries or millenia later, we can still recognise in them the images and ideas peculiar to those cultures. Thus, a native Indian story from North America stands apart from a European folktale in its theme, structure and pacing. Not just the mapping of relationships characteristic of a society, but also its cosmology and its ways of recognising the basic challenges of life are reflected in a story that has evolved in it. When we tell the story we have chosen out of the vast repertoire of the world's story heritage, we participate in the psychosocial universe of the culture in which the story arose and acquired its popular form. Thus, by telling a story, we invoke the culture that gave it birth. And not just briefly for the duration it takes to tell the story, but in a more lasting sense as well, for the reason that a well-told story is likely to be remembered, especially if it is told several times.

Stories coming from the same cultural or geographical region may have a remarkably different texture of symbolic meanings, depending on the historical phase in the development of the culture in which they find their present-day form. Many of the *Panchatantra* stories—like the one analysed above—represent the instinct for survival, imprinted as they are by a culture in which the fear that power might be used without justice was common. The *Jataka* tales, by contrast, represent a world of relationships and meanings structured around a benign hope. Apparently, they acquired their form and fame during a period of deep social and political churning in the Indian society. The world represented in the *Jataka* stories, more so the world they propose, is a benign place in which the potential for transformation is so great that it keeps every situation fluid and dynamic.

Another striking difference can be seen between the anthropomorphic world of the *Panchatantra*, in which human instincts and perspectives use the mask of animal characters, and the *Jataka* world where the human, the non-human, and the non-living intermesh, representing the state of 'interbeing'. Realisation rather than retribution is the favoured narrative solution of the *Jataka*. Cleverness does not count for much; rather, it is the will to change and to see things differently that creates the hope of a solution to the problem posed in a story. This is obviously an altogether different moral universe from the one represented in the *Panchatantra*, though both are equally significant members of India's great story heritage. The stunning diversity of stances towards the basic questions of life we see in these and other story traditions is also a testimony to the pluralism inherent in Indian civilisation.

The scope of this discussion can be easily extended by including in it the story traditions of other cultures. Each story tradition conveys the defining impact of geography and social conditions, and also of the historical experiences a culture has undergone. This is why, we are able to distinguish a French, a Scandinavian, and a Russian tale without being told about its place of origin. The notion of a monolithic Western culture disappears when we recognise the diversity of formal features and themes in European story traditions. A similar thing would happen if we subjected the popularly held concept of an Eastern or Oriental culture to a scrutiny based on the story traditions, for example, of India, China, and Japan.

The diversity of cultural content and worldviews notwithstanding, all storytelling traditions represent an oral culture of communication. In a world in which literary and electronic media dominate our concept of communication, it is hardly surprising that we rarely worry about, or show respect for, morality as culture. In a literate social universe, those who depend on oral communication are referred to, derisively, as illiterates. They are inevitably regarded as being unfortunate, even handicapped, constituting an impediment to the nation's progress. Any attempt to highlight the value of the oral is labelled as being romantic and wistful. Yet, a great deal of life continues to present challenges that can only be met orally. Listening to a story temporarily places the child in an orally organised culture. The least we can expect from this experience is that it will supplement, and provide a counterbalancing element in the child's educational growth in a literacy-dominated culture. As an organising principle, communication imparts immediacy and directness to human relationships, both of which are important ingredients of a democratic order. Even if universalisation of literacy seems more visibly related to equality and democratic participation under present-day circumstances, oral communication must be granted the role of creating an eidos in which egalitarian relationship might find an opportunity to develop. When stories are told and heard with pleasure and habitual attention to detail, a culture not altogether irrelevant for modern democracies is resuscitated.

□

Language Teaching at Primary Level

—Binodanand Jha

We treat language as a medium for expressing our ideas and experiences, but apart from being a source of communication, language is useful for us in many ways. When we contact another person, society or world language becomes medium for communication but when we think within ourselves, experience something, do debate or see dream the it gets a new role for us. We also take help from language in connection with Memory, Visualisation, Debate, Happiness, Annoyance and Affection and with it form a glimpse in our inner mind. Language has got a greater role with the children, which increases from time to time.

Language is the basis and source for spiritual and mental development of children—for this it is necessary that children should learn language in natural course. By natural or normal course we mean that they should use language in simple way. They should have meaningful reference. Teachers will have to design and create meaningful references so that children can learn in normal course how to visualise and debate—without hesitation, can talk on poetry and story.

Teacher's reaction on the language used by children play a vital role in development of language within them. Negative reaction, on the one hand, obstructs children's language and the other, the positive reaction brings new possibilities of development.

Language is a flexible means which we can convert as per our life's requirement and circumstances. Use of language in flexible manner decide to a greater extent how we will tackle different situations of life. Language affects our expectations.

It is because of the flexibility of language that any person can write letter to different persons (say father, son, wife etc.) using the same context—there the language changes as per the person. If he writes to his supervisor the language changes as per the context.

Reference: The Soldiers and Officers of Army communicate during Parade or War in a different language whereas in Society the same soldier uses normal language, meaning thereby that a single person uses different types of language as per the need and requirement. Persons in trade and Profession use language in accordance with their trade and profession. This is only possible because of flexible nature of language.

The Limitations of Text Books

We know that children have large vocabulary before coming to school. They are fully aware of their surroundings and environment. They know the festivals, stories, songs and poems. A peculiar type of language capability is what they possess.

It is our misfortune that under the education system language used in the school and text books is different from what they use with friends and at home. Generally the language used in the School is not used outside the boundary wall of School. In the School, teachers, because of systems generated compulsions proceed without knowing the past knowledge, understanding, visualisation and feelings of children by teaching them in the artificial language. Here the children get a big blow. They ask themselves : what they have learn earlier or were taught earlier was wrong?

This is a blow on their visualisation and freedom of expression. They become deviated from the aim of learning and enjoying. The artificial language in itself has got no special attribute. In such circumstances we will have to think how sensitive we are toward the language used by the children in Primary Classes.

The chapters taken in text books are not relevant to children. This is not liked by them. So, they lose interest for studying the language. Poems and Stories are taught only with the intention that they can reply.

By this they do not get opportunity to visualise, opening from inside. Studies which is a process of joy becomes a burden on them. There are so many decided points in curriculam which they know before coming to school. Incorporating that is only a waste of time both for teaches and students.

Methods used for language teaching in the School totally negate known knowledge. Ignoring past knowledge means ignoring complete personality of a child. In such circumstances children will lose interest in the School. Can the language teaching be not attached to their immediate environment and interest?

Instead of understanding the language and its expression -concentration is more on memorising answers to the questions given in the chapter. Leepi, Vartani, good handwriting and grammar arc the key points for teaching of language in school.

With the point of view of importance, misbalanced distribution of allotted time does not permit students to play with words, go deep into it, experiencing it. If this is not, why should we do?

A child when he goes to the school uses those words which he uses at home such as—'Ghaila', 'Mai', 'Kukkur', 'Gitti', 'Gachh' etc. If the child uses 'Gachh' in place of 'tree' we should understand that he fully understands tree. In the beginning he may be allowed to say Gachh in place of tree, later on he will understand that tree and 'Gachh' are the same.

Teachers in the class should talk to children to know the words used in their language at home, then to frame those into school's language.

Language Teaching : How?

While teaching language, teachers should create such an environment the enables children to think, understand and express. Their mind-brain start saying—A picture of kite flying in the sky be shown to child with questions such as what you are seeing in the picture? In which direction is air flowing? What may be the time of the day? Why only boys are flying kite, Why not girls?

Inquisitiveness has got a greater role to plan in the learning of language. For this, certain subjects, incidents, play, the surprising events be dwelled upon so that the children can start visualising what, how and why. With this the question will come to their mind and this will be helpful to the children.

In language learning useful references are important for developing language ability. Such references should be suitable to their level, experience and environment. No reference should be taken which may frighten the child or make them feel pressure—Every opportunity be given to Children to talk freely in the class. Deliberation suited to its environment be done. Child's temperament, memory, expression- in fact everything be taken importantly to see up to what level they have understood. Attributes of language are listening, talking, reading, writing – all of them can only be learnt by doing. Correct pronunciation does not mean reading, instead to know the meaning is reading. Prior to teaching writing, Children be shown pictures and figures to identify sounds. Drawing figures on sand, moving fingers on words, putting thread into needle, separating dry pulses with dry rice which were placed together in a bowl-develops balance in the muscle.

For children, moving from letter to word is very complicated and impracticable as well. It would be appropriate if letters are introduced through words. Child is familiar with all the words such as 'Kalam', 'Kamal'. In the beginning exercise be undertaken through audio. Children by continuous use of the words will know the sound.

Practice is very important for the exercise of learning of language. If any child is to be taught listening and speaking it be taken up with interesting stories, surprising events etc. Environment be created with lovely poems and songs.

Deliberations are also important, but in our school, we think children talking to each other is inappropriate. Class with complete silence is known as disciplined and purposeful. In fact conversation between Students and debates play an important role in the learning of language. They exchange views by supplementing it to so many facts, experiences and knowledge. Every child tries to communicate what he wanted to tell. For this, speaker and listener exchange why and what etc because of which children make themselves effective orator and develop linguistic ability.

In the class room language and other subjects have close relation. This is because language is the medium for exchange of views and knowledge—so its efficiency is required for teaching. For knowledge of any subject efficiency in language is needed.

Language upto Which Level?

This is an important question. It is our belief that text book is a material for language teaching. Text Books are used to take children up to a decided level but this should never be thought that development of language is contained in the Text Book. In fact the boundaries of language are very wide. Still there is scope for its enhancement. A book should be taught in such a way that the child gets ability to understand and use beyond that.

In this course the process of evaluation goes on continuously. By evaluation only we could know how much the child has learned. On this basis only the other methods of learning and teaching are decided.

The various aspects of teaching such as listening, speaking, reading, writing, understanding, inquisitiveness and exercise be kept in mind while doing evaluation and this brings naturality in learning process. This be kept in mind that language is a technique (skill) oriented subject—so what according to you should be the type of evaluation?

Listening: Child through listening understands the incidents, poetry and story and expresses his opinion. His evaluation will be on listening. If he expresses understanding of expressions and meaning—then it can be said that listening ability has increased.

Speaking: Children are anxious to talk about their personal experiences. They need encouragement. If they are provided with the opportunity they can be evaluated on their experience in school.

Reading: To believe that seeing the word and its pronunciation is reading – is a myth. The important thing is to bring out its meaning. Many a time it is our complaint that a particular child does not understand even after reading. By this it is thought that reading and understanding are different whereas the wider definition of reading has an object of understanding. Therefore without understanding, reading has got no value.

Writing: Many a time a child can read but is not able to write. When a child can write what other is speaking and then can read them—he may be evaluated on that.

In the same manner children by repeating, experiencing and visualising get meaning. We conclude that the child has learnt. Professor Krishna Kumar wrote in his book 'Child, Language and Teacher' that every child in the world whatever may be his mother tongue uses the language for certain objectives. A big objective is understanding the world-and for this objective language acts as a better tool. So long as we are unable to see the language from Childs' eye, we shall not be able to play our role as a good teacher.

Our responsibility as a teacher is clear. During deliberations, reading, writing, singing, playing in the drama we will have to prepare an environment so that the child can connect life's experiences and incidents with language.

Language Class

In the normal situation children learn naturally. The environment in the class should be normal and free—for this the teacher will have to keep mindful relations with Children, giving importance to their feelings and wishes. To make language's class effective, the following needs to be kept in mind:

(1) All children should have participation in the class

(2) Every Child should have freedom to talk

(3) Mother tongue be given respect and appropriate place

(4) Originality be also kept in mind, Class will be alive and natural if teachers are effective communicators.

Prime Thoughts of Language Teaching

- Language is the medium for expressing our views.
- Language apart from communication is a tool for our thinking, experiencing and dreaming.
- Thinking, understanding, debating, estimating and analysing are the important aspects of development of language.
- Language's context and place are important.
- Children easily express their views through their language of environment which in normal terms are known as 'Boli'.
- When the pressure is made on a child for using for using pure and standard language the power of his expression is hindered and becomes weak.
- A teacher has a pivotal role in children's Language learning. A teacher can create such experience in the

class which can take a child from home's language to school's language in an interesting way.

- Effective activities for development of language may be—to connect Children from their known and interesting contexts using pictures, stories, poems and drama, debate.
- Visualisation and seeing things from their own eyes are important.
- Teacher's reaction on the use of language play a vital role in language development. Teacher's negative reaction may cause hindrance in absorbing language by a child.
- Teachers should create such circumstances which can enhance the skills already possessed.
- Claiming that reading is an accepted procedure for learning is absolutely wrong.
- For children moving from letter to word is cumbersome and impracticable as well. It would be appropriate if they are taught letters from words, because in the beginning he sees the entire thing.
- For writing in the beginning focus be not placed on good handwriting. Similarly grammatical definitions be not imposed.

□

A School's Said Thought

—**Gyandeo Mani Tripathi**

Till now much has been written, published and read on me. Right from illustrious educationists to unknown education servers—all by their own way explained and made efforts for defining me. If I ponder into History I see my past in the institutions way back Harappa Culture, when by mixing Copper and Tin Kansa was prepared or covered drainage were connected with civilisation and human life, but now being totally free from all these things I want to see in my own way. So now in this 21st Century I am breaking my silence.

Now I am a Government Primary School. My present has roots in the past which has Harrapa Society Ghatika, Charan, Math-Vihar, Maqtab – Madrasa and the schools aided by East India Company. Now I can not tell out of them whose culture is alive in me. My truth today is that I am a Government Primary School which is running in a Village named Nagadaha for the last 100 years. Birth means establishment which was in 1885. In the same year Congress was established by Hume—surprised to see a new person. Oh ! you are Master Saheb. I knew that it would be you, otherwise how far I am concerned with these facts and figures and what is the meaning of my observing World's greatest incidents. This has been the habit of literate persons who never under lived important local incidents and if at all they made efforts it was in the context of national or international events. It seems local history has got no independent existence. Master Saheb, gives importance to local activities as well. You may have talked repeatedly about the establishment of Congress for competing in the competitive Examinations but you are here for the last three years not knowing the date of establishment of your school and its background—whose existence is necessary for your secured future.

Anyway leave these things. See two villagers have come to attend you. In the available Voter List, their names, father's name is correct, but their sex has been changed. They are male but shown as female. Looking about of age 40-50 but shown 6 years. Go, do the correction and list will go on and teaching will be suspended. —what to say when students are not coming. I am not happy. I know that these children will be interfering in the Scheduled work of mother and father. I cannot do anything as this is the Government's order. However in the democracy voter list must be corrected.

I was thinking that I will utilise the time for witting my statements (Bayan) but every time inspection by Commissioner or Committee and its recommendations has not allowed registration of my views, also this time my teaching disrupted but now I have decided that I will give my statement (Bayan) – despite facing all difficulties.

I was telling that 10 years back at the right hand corner of the village I was respectfully placed. The picture of this village in my memory does not show any body proficient in modern education. Yes, because of local 'Math' there were few people knowing traditional Sanskrit Education and few having studied from Maktab—were capable to teach Urdu. For doing local work the language used was 'Kaithi'. There were Zamindars who were collecting tax and interested in exploitation. Local people were doing harvesting which was means for livelihood. Literates were respected but there was no wave that everybody should study. People from all the caste were residing in the village. Between Hindu-Muslim the common language was Bhojpuri. Atmosphere was free from religious tension. Mostly people were barefooted. At that time no house was with concrete. One or two houses which were with one or two brick -walls were also having roof of Khaprail (made of red soil). Mostly people have not even seen the British Currency. But still then all the necessities were available in the Village. Market at Malahi was famous. Means of transport was Bullock Cart. There was rumour that somebody purchased Bicycle. Many people were using boat in Gandak. People were afraid of British Army. In the nearby Sirahi Kothi Nilha Saheb was residing. People were afraid while going in front of Kothi. And if they passed by it was without Pagadi, Cap or Umbrella. By and large my establishment was done in such environment in a Phoos (a type of grass) house.

Thoughbehindmyestablishmentwastherecommendation of Hunter Commission(188 -83) "that primary education be entrusted to Local Bodies,. such tradition was there already which was seen by Adams(18 4-33). At that time there was great enthusiasm for my establishment. Required materials, labour, pathway to produce came from different people/corner which created my very small building where the children were to be taught by Teacher. In the beginning teachers came from Chhapra. Leaving their own people, and home, they provided education which was the greatest duty. School started under the supervision of Teacher. In the beginning a number of misconceptions were spread, referring to them now will lead to unnecessary disputes. Leaving them will be the best. With the sincere efforts of the first teacher children of the village started coming to the school. Up to the end of 19th Century only those children came to School who did not have any work at home. Thus only few could complete even the primary education. Girls did not come to School.

With the inception of the new century, changes were evident. DPI changed with the change of Lord and School Inspectors were also changed. I was also changed and my place was also changed. Now I came in between those who were named 'Harijan' by Gandhiji. School Building was constructed at the eastern corner of the Village. Yadavas, Boat Man-mallahs and Harijan people were residing. I am not saying that unaccountability was not there. It was there but there was no hindrance during construction on that basis: why I have been brought from the area of the higher caste whereas even then children were mostly from their home, but there was no teacher for 40 years from the higher caste. Teachers were from nearby Villages so they were coming on time and going back in the evening. One teacher was from this Village whose arrangement for stay and food was made by Villagers. Though there are many incidents which if I refer to will take hundreds of pages. So that detail I will give in my autobiography (Autobiography of A School). As my submission is spontaneous so only important incidents are out-lined. For the sake of convenience I am dividing them into 3 parts—(1) Period of my establishment (the end of 19th Century) (2) Pre Independence (3) Post Independence. I have up to now told you the story of my establishment, that means we have come to 20th Century. Now I am having rooms – brick walls and Khaprail roof. A small play ground is there, but no arrangement for drinking water was there. When the children were thirsty they would go to the house of Achaldeo-Kamaldeo Raut where the ladies happily provided them the drinking water.

Now few Children were getting ready to go to the Middle School. Some of them even went to High School at Motihari. A new wave was flowing in the Country. Demand for Independence was taking momentum. At that time News Papers were not available in the Village. Only one person was having Radio – which he played some time with great pomp and show. Therefore news was not available. Teachers were going to head quarters seldom. So the news from Calcutta-Delhi came through mouth, which was available with great mixing. Residents of the village were having nothing to do with it, but few people from this village were now not only crossing the District but State also. Our teachers were in the employment of British Government, so they were avoiding such people. On one day there was great news that one Mahatma has come and British People are sending him to Jail because he is propagating that Britishers by doing violence are harassing the farmers. This has created a great ruckus. The entire District assembled at Motihari Court to hear Mohandas Karamchand Gandhi. From this village four – five ex- students were there. I was happy to see them there. After all it is the responsibility of school to provide its Students the capability to decide and take steps as per the circumstances. I feel proud on the decision taken by my students. It was marvellous saying by Mahatma Gandhi that he, guided by his inner soul, has decided to disobey the administration's orders. These people were telling that he has been invited here by Raj Kumar Sukul of Satwaria (Sathi). Now a new centre for information was opened. Any body going to Bettiah—Motihari was also bringing one or other news.

My activities were going on. Then it was Child Class. Class was divided into A B C. Class 3rd was also in the same form. 'Manohar Pothi' came into existence then. Printed book with the name 'Manohar Pothi' was the only book available. Everything was in it—vocabulary, Pahadas, Gintee, Savaiya and Dedha. In the senior classes students were studying Hindi and Mathematics. First the news of Village and District then of State and of British Government were to be read. There was the concept of Tappa and Pargana. My tappa was Sakhwa and Pargana was Majhaua. Morning prayers began with – "He Prabhu Ananddata Gyan Hamko Dijiye, Lijiye Hamko Sharan Me, Ham Sadachari Bane..." There was light exercise and then children would go to their respective classes. Child class and A in one, B, C in one, 4th, 5th in one. Teachers were only 3. During last 50 years for only few days 5 teachers were there. Out of them one was the Head Master. So there were joint classes. In the first period oral work was there. Small children were writing on Slates and 4th, 5th Class students were writing on paper using Pencil. For all Students above Class 2nd were required to do fine writing. Ink tablet was mixed with water in

Ink Pot and by cutting a wood (Sarkanda) in the shape of a nib Children use it for fine writing (Sulekh). Children themselves were preparing Ink and wooden nib. They knew that this ink would not dry quickly so they use soil for drying it. It was their bloating paper.

Because writing and reading was mostly on Slate, so it was seen by Teacher for making corrections. In those days rush of students was not such which may involve full day of the teacher to control them. In the joint classes there were not more than 5 children. During Tiffin time children would go to their home. Some of them would not come back—the teacher would keep track of them. Education at that time was not so humane. So teachers were having a stick which they were using. Generally this stick was known as Dukh Haran among the children. Children were afraid of this, but teachers were not using them when not required. Those who were using it unnecessarily were known as 'Markhanda Teacher'.

When the teachers are remembered I recall some of my old teachers namely Ramyad Ram, Ramashish Rai, Jamir Hassan, Ramashish Dube, Sinhasan Prasad, Binda Prasad, Satyanarain Giri, Padhya Master Saheb, Niralaji etc. The one teacher whom I remember most can be identified from far because of his small height, whitish complexion, Pyjama up to just below knees, white small cap on head—Language like a child (intentionally). Jamir Hassan in lead and following him the children. Coming to the school walking from 4 kms. and then bringing Children to school. Meeting parents, elderly people of village, after greeting them informing them about the work done by School, but never making any complaint about Children. If anybody complained he would tell no child is bad. We are bad and are trying to make our child like that. Don't tell rubbish about our children. Jamir Hassan was a great supporter of the children, who knew all good qualities of the Children and loved them very much.

Jamir Hassan means 'Chhotka Maulavi Saheb'. All children were admirer of him. Today if from students Jamir Hassan's remembrance, memories are collected it will be a voluminous book with characteristics of one of its type. There will not be any Student - boy or girl, who does not remember Jamir Saheb's classes and this remembrance is not without any reason. Jamir Hassan was a teacher with great insight. He was teaching children in class I. With the playful tactics he imparted all the things to students. He did not require any book for teaching. Entire course and its structure was in his mind. Those days village children were playing Gullidanda and Kabbadi vigorously. Chhotka Maulavi Saheb knew the minds of children, thus children were able to know Mathematics-while playing Gullidanda. The play was beginning with the size of Gulli and Danda. Gulli should be one fourth of Danda. One child places the Gulli in small hole in the earth and throws it through Danda. Now when the Gulli falls the distance from hole to this place is measured. 1, 10, 0 and more—through this the child is learning measurement. There are two groups of children playing. One group scored 136 and the other 83, teacher says that everybody will remember their own calculation. Here with decreasing trend children are learning Mathematics. Everybody will have to remember because when the play will be resumed a day after then it should be known. One who is not able to tell calculation will not play. No child would like to ignore such an opportunity for playing. Everyone knows his calculation. Few children were capable of throwing three to four times. This provides them opportunity for knowing multiplication.

Similarly it was Jamir Hassan's Kabbadi. When the entire state was playing by shouting Kabbadi—Kabbadi in one breath Jamir Hassan's children will shout—hundred, ninety nine, ninety eight, ninety seven—sixty, fifty nine—thirty six, thirty five and many in descending/decreasing order will count from 100 to 1. In this way children learnt decreasing counting. At the time of closure when children recited decreasing counting, the entire environment was full of that. Many new tactics and methods were devised by Chhotka Maulavi Saheb, which were not described in any Book. Two groups are playing Kabbadi. A child of of one group crosses the line with 100, 99 – trying to touch a member of other group, but up to reaching 40 he loses command over breath and tries to go back—another member of the group can cross line by shouting 39, 38, 37. Only condition is that before the first one loses the breath the second one should pick up the counting thread.

The teaching by Chhotka Maulavi Saheb was the same. All the things in singing tone. When he arrives in class a few children sing '*Tiffin wali batiya bhor padi jala*' (Not remembering the issue of tiffin)—few have not come back yesterday after the tiffin. Children by this singing are reminding him. He calls a child who did not come after tiffin yesterday. Chotka Maulavi with his crossed finger touches stomach of Child saying shall I remove your ears. Entire class laughed. His art of teaching was excellent and was knowing numerous Stories. Students loved him greatly. He remained with me for 36 years. Everyday was unique. I know that degree holders are not enjoying his praise, he was only Middle Pass. A research may be done on him as to how such ideas came to a person who was not very educated and how he was having so much of insight and faculty of excellent visualisation.

But that night was very dreadful when I learnt that in a land dispute my beloved teacher Jamir Hassan was murdered. This price he got for laughing and speaking happiness entire life. I could not get into it. Wept for a long. His Students who got this news were stunned and pained, but next day it is felt that he is singing slowly '*Nak me ungli, kan me lakdi, matkar, matkar*'. His date of birth and date of death both are remembered by me but there is no practice as yet for celebrating them. But I may have to start that. Neither school nor his relatives have got his picture, but my heart has a clear picture of him. If I will be able to get a room in his name at the school. Now greeding that a similar man may come again to the School.

□

How to Teach Mathematics

—Binodanand Jha

In Primary Education, Mathematics is a compulsory subject. It starts from Class-I which goes up to Class-X. There are many beliefs regarding Mathematics in the children and Teachers. Many a time continuance of Children in any school is seen in the context of teaching and learning of Mathematics. We have done some efforts on that. It was discussed formally and informally with Children and Teachers of schools. During the course of discussions following important facts have emerged:

(1) Mathematics is not a lively subject. Its contents are mostly invisible (*amurta*) so there is a feeling of fear among children and a few Teachers.

(2) To understand it, a special type of mind is required. It means that those who have such type of mind will take interest in Mathematics.

(3) The image of Mathematics Teacher is also different in the mind of Children. They are seen as of serious nature-awarding less marks.

When we go deep regarding the questions given above it seems necessary to ponder over following points:

Connecting Invisible with Visible: Mathematics is a Invisible subject. It is its speciality but at the primary stage children are to be taught—Invisible is to be explained through – say – if you say 5 it has got no impact on mind, but if you add

5 Bananas, 5 Goats it makes sense to Children. Mathematics should be taught in a playful manner and with concrete examples.

Such examples can be taken from the experience of children. One incident can be proved through many examples such as 5 Oranges + 7 Oranges = 12 Oranges. 7 Books + 9 Books = 16 Books, 4 Bags + 6 Bags = 10 Bags. This needs continuous exercise.

Childrens prior Knowledge and Experience should be the Basis: A child knows so many things before entering the school. He has got experience and knowledge of less-excess, small-big, collecting things, measuring, counting, keeping them in Box. If the teacher uses all these things in teaching then Mathematics will be easy for children. It may happen that at child's home there are different units of measurement such as Kanwa, Pauva, Ser, Paseri, Man, Bitta, Hath, Gaj etc. but these can be taken along the knowledge obtained from books.

Importance of Assumptions in Mathematics: Generally we tend to remember rules or principles of Mathematics in Class—no—where it is explained why such rules have been framed. As a result the Child remains not introduced to entire assumptions. While teaching Mathematics establishing assumptions is an important step. From the beginning, assumptions coupled with different examples are to be placed in place. In case we proceed without this the Child will be able to solve simple questions but when there are complications he will become nervous.

Assumptions should not be formed in haste. When exercises for Mathematics are made without assumptions the subject becomes difficult as well as tedious. Children commit mistakes one by one then think that Mathematics is 'hard' and difficult. Before forming assumption, teachers should verify children's past knowledge. This past knowledge should become basis—with which we can go ahead.

For example before learning assumption of multiplication, it should be seen whether he knows assumption for addition. It is easy to carry forward assumption of multiplication through the one for addition. It is easy to proceed from known to unknown --which also develops interest among the children.

For establishing assumption exercise is important. Take one example—In case assumption regarding Chair is to be given we can tell its merits but if only a Chair is shown – its assumption will not be complete. Mostly Chairs have four legs but Revolving Chairs have only one. Some have design for keeping arm but some do not have. Only by telling definition and few merits assumption is not complete. After many exercises the Child can say that this is a Steel Chair and the other is of Plastic.

Attitude Toward Mistakes: A new thinking toward mistakes committed be given. Generally when Teachers and Parents detect a mistake they immediately start scolding the child. For example

$$\begin{array}{r} 38 \\ +\ 22 \\ \hline 510 \end{array} \qquad \begin{array}{r} 35 \\ +\ 37 \\ \hline 612 \end{array} \qquad \begin{array}{r} 26 \\ +\ 25 \\ \hline 411 \end{array}$$

Teacher can give ZERO marks for this but this shows that the Child knows addition of first number but he is committing mistake in second number. Every mistake is not ignorance but a step toward learning. Mistakes show that child knows something and is not fully ignorant. If the Teacher is capable he can understand where child is continuously committing mistakes—by correcting them the child can learn Mathematics easily and rapidly. Generally the Mathematics teachers do not take mistakes as a helping tool, they rather show a negative attitude, which disheartens a Child and makes him disinterested in Mathematics. It has also to be kept in mind that adults and children have different methods of their learning. Therefore Teachers and Parents should relook into their attitude toward mistakes committed by a child.

Procedure and Result in the Mathematics: In the Mathematical learning, procedure and results are to be debated. Generally we see the answer and arrive at a conclusion that it has been solved correctly. But only getting result is not important. In Mathematics- procedure helps us in solving questions; when the procedure is wrong and the answer which we got is correct—it is only a coincidence. Whereas with correct procedure the correct answer is a definite outcome. Procedure should be given importance and not the answer.

Role of Mathematics Teachers: All the above points are attached to the role of teacher. Apart from this Mathematics teachers have got responsibility to place the subject in simple manner. Child be given opportunity to ask questions and it be taken in positive manner.

In case we can make the Child inquisitive and to tackle the problem they can solve hard questions also. Probably it is because of this that those children who are selling Coconut, Vegetable or Fruit can do the calculation quickly. No doubt they may not be proficient in bookish Mathematics but they can quickly say what will be the price for 750 gm Lady Finger @ 20/- per Kg. Mathematics has also got its beauty. It provides a special logical power to the mind. These should be attached with life's experiences meant for proceeding with the studies in Class. Solving Questions on Black Board will not suffice.

How to make Weak and Lagging Behind Children Understand: In the area of Teaching we have an idea that a particular child will not be able to learn Mathematics. It may be that environment at his home, and his social, financial position are not congenial for the situation. May be he is coming to the school after helping his mother-father at home, he may not be getting any help in Studies. Every Child has got different pace of learning. Many children who are weak in the initial classes, get good results afterwards. We should keep a concept of continuing possibilities.

Summarily, following things should be in Mathematics Class:

1. Opportunity should be there for self learning.

There should be freedom of speed for learning.

3. Every Child should get opportunity to choose his own procedure and its use.
4. Relation between Student and Teacher should be fearless and of belongingness.
5. Teacher should try to correct the mistake rather than scold the Child.
6. Activities and teaching material should be used for assumption.
7. Importance should be given to the past knowledge and experience of the Child.
8. Assessment should not be valued as per marks obtained but it should depend on how much the Child has understood.

We have tried to put forth certain concrete suggestions for procedure to be adopted during teaching of Mathematics. Now a practical approach be taken in the Class. Persons related with teaching of Mathematics should take viewpoint for an integrated approach on teaching and children.

□

What is a 'Good' Classroom?

—Subir Shukla

A classroom is essentially defined by the nature of interaction among its participants, that is, children and teachers, and occasionally community members as well.

It is often said that most teachers are not interested in teaching. Hence, that point in trying to identify what makes for a 'good' classroom, especially for teachers, does not arise at all! Just a waste of time it is said.

Why bother about it?

The people who argue thus also tend to be full of platitudes about the dos and don'ts that a teacher should follow. They tend to overlook the fact that the typical government school teacher has a very difficult situation – a shifting population of children who are at different levels, with home conditions that do not always support education, with having to handle more than one language and more than one class! Naturally, teachers end up finding much of the advice given to them as merely a pile of someone else's dreams that they have to try to live up to under impossible circumstances.

To my mind, therefore, the question 'what is a good classroom?' is closely linked with what is possible and not just what is desirable. When teachers find that a good classroom is actually possible, more and more of them will actually try to improve their classrooms. Why? Because they will find in it much more fun and satisfaction than continuing to live the same humdrum life as before.

What is a classroom?

So, to start with, what do we mean by 'classroom'? In fact, it was a teacher who provided the real answer to this, during a discussion on the future of a foreign-funded project, on whether it would continue or not, and what would happen to schools if it did not. This teacher said, "Nothing! Nothing will happen to the school merely because the foreign funding stops. It is a mistake to think that a school is in building, and books and doors and windows. It is, actually, what happens between my children and me. People can come and remove the doors or break the building, but nobody can touch the real thing – that is, what happens between my children and me!"

Thus, a classroom is really a learning situation, the physical aspect of which, though important in its own way, is not as crucial as the emotional, intellectual, social and cultural one. A classroom is essentially defined by the nature of interaction among its participants, that is, children and teachers, and occasionally others as well (e.g., community members). By itself, the physical aspect can help but not determine this interaction. The focus in this note, therefore, is more on this interaction rather than on things that need financial resources.

Work less!

Some years ago, I visited a 'model' school that was implementing what was considered to be 'activity-based teaching'. A teacher from this school complained that such teaching was very, very tiring! On going to his classroom, I found that the teacher himself was doing all the signing, action, and so on, while the children sat and watched! Naturally, it was very tiring.

In many ways, even in the traditional classroom, this is what we end up doing much of the time. We think out everything for the child, provide all the answers, spoon feed much of the time and believe that we are very hardworking! Often, even if something is already known to children, we teach the same thing over again without bothering to find out whether children can do it on their own or not.

So, the first step in getting to a good classroom is: work less! Avoid doing for children what they should be doing for themselves. See yourself as a facilitator rather than a dispenser of knowledge. Make use of their previous knowledge and understanding (and there is plenty of that, believe me). Create room for students to arrive at their own understanding. Instead of wasting time on issues already known to them, identify areas where they really need support and concentrate on them.

Create tasks and beginnings

How can you get around to working less? By finding interesting tasks, which children would like to work upon on their own, leaving you free to offer support where it is needed.

All children are naturally more active than passive. They love challenges, and working on situations that 'move' from one point to another (e.g., games, or making things, or enacting something, or solving a problem). They also find it fun to work with each other, and help each other. Make use of these tendencies to create interesting tasks that you start children off on (as against doing it all for them), and then support them as they complete these tasks.

For example, if you want to teach counting, set up dice games where children are required to count (can you think of a few examples of this?). Or fill up a small container with pebbles, ask them to guess how many there are, and then count to verify. Or, if you are teaching language, create card games where they pull out letter cards randomly and then make words. Or give them a riddle about a character in a story and then read the story on their own (rather than having it read aloud by you) to find the answer. Or, if you are teaching environmental studies, ask students to find out about leaves by making a collection, sorting it, and answering interesting questions. Or ask them to devise an experiment to counter or justify a claim you might have made (e.g., a needle can be made to float).

In all this, your role really is that of identifying tasks or activities that:

- students will find interesting and challenging (that is, they will be possible, but not too easy for their level),
- have a purpose for them (which may be different from the purpose they have for you!), and
- are related to curricular objectives you are focussing on.

Once you have presented the task, children start on them and you offer help only where it is needed.

Finally, once the tasks are over, your role is that of enabling reflection on what has just been experienced, in order to consolidate it in terms of learning. Thus children are not learning by memorising, but by thinking on their own and coming to their own understanding.

As you can see, a good classroom is very different from the one where the teacher is doing the talking and pushing and driving much of the time. It is infinitely more relaxing to create interesting tasks and watch students doing them, with minimum help from you. All this, of course, does not happen in one go. You have to start carefully with what can actually be done before moving on into a situation where your class has children working on their own for a great part of the time.

Don't allow yourself to get bored

Even the most interesting tasks, done repeatedly, begin to wear out and soon stop being interesting. And then loss of interest on the learners' part results in loss of learning. So, what is being suggested is not merely doing a few apparently interesting tasks over and over again. There is a need to build in a natural amount of variety in what is being done. In the absence of variety, learning suffers.

A new activity might need to be repeated in more or less the same manner in the beginning. But, very soon, variations in it would be needed. For example, a guessing game where the teacher gives hints for children to guess on the basis of (e.g., I am a plant, whose leaves you eat), after some time would have to be done differently (e.g., asking children to make the riddle, or switching on to animals or gases). Instead of asking children to answer as a whole class, they could be divided into small groups or even be required to work individually. Clues could be given in writing, or children be asked to pick up cards on which a word is written or picture drawn, on the basis of which they may have to frame the riddle. In fact, it is very easy to make an activity easier or more difficult depending on the level, background and interests of children, something that is not always possible with the typical textbook lesson.

As you can see, whether a session of 40 minutes or a whole day, there can be sufficient variety across the period, enabling children to retain their interest. At the same time, since all children do not necessarily learn in the same way, this variety enables all children to find a means suited to their particular way of learning.

What all this implies is that the old system – of teaching the whole class in the same way the whole time with the same material – is not very appropriate. In an activity-oriented classroom, it should be possible for variety, and even for different children (say in different groups) doing what is appropriate for them. Such self-learning phases during a day or session provide the teacher an opportunity to help those children who might need such help more.

Discover how rich you are!

Make a list of all those things that can be found in or around your school, e.g., benches, polythene bags, seeds, sticks, pebbles, charts, leaves, sand, old calendars strings, and countless other things. You'll find that most of them can serve as learning material for something or the other you might want to teach. For example, leaves help in classification and mathematical operations, sticks in seriation and spatial skills, and so on. The best part is that they are all free, and you don't even have to make an effort to get them yourself – asking children to collect such material is part of the learning process.

In addition, there are plenty of things you and children can make together, which can be used for a variety of learning purposes. For example, masks, clay toys, picture charts, flash cards of all kinds, and so on.

Finally, many of you will be lucky enough to have material that has been supplied (e.g., kits for science or mathematics, or library books, etc.) or even be given a certain amount for purchase of materials. Earlier, teachers used to be worried that if any material is spoilt, they would have to pay for it, and this resulted in all this material being kept in cupboards or trunks. But now, authorities have realised that material is actually to be used! Hence, torn books or weathered material are no longer considered disastrous. Use it as well and as much as you would like to.

In interaction with such material, children learn through the use of their sense organs and through the dynamic manipulation of material from one state to another, as in arranging or making a model or solving a problem and the like.

Thus, it is no more true to say that there is a shortage of material, and in a good classroom, one would expect to see plenty of it – in children hands rather than being displayed on the wall!

Get children to run the class.

Ah, but how can the teacher do all this? By looking upon children as team members who play a role in running the class, rather than as a 'herd to be managed'. One critical assumption here is that once children have purposeful tasks to do, they do not need 'discipline' (you have to try this out before doubting this statement!). In an atmosphere of freedom where children can talk, ask questions, and collaborate in completing a task. It is usual to find that they are able to take decisions, handle responsibility, and are eager to support the teacher in as many ways as possible. This includes handling material collection, distribution and storage; helping other children if needed; maintaining discipline on their own. This last one is facilitated best if the whole class (that is, teachers and children together) makes commonly agreed upon ground rules for functioning, including deciding upon the consequences of violating them. In such a situation, it is common to find that children rarely need to be made to do something. Instead, they come on their own to find out what they should do.

Of course, the difficulty arises when the teacher himself violates the agreed upon ground rules. If he willingly accepts the consequences, he sends a strong message of equality and participation to his children, and discipline is really no problem.

In a good classroom, therefore, we would expect to see everyone working as a group, having both a say and a responsibility too.

Plan like it's a meal

Naturally, such a classroom would not come about on its own. It needs to be planned for. Again, you'll find many people saying that teachers cannot really plan. And once again, this is something that is simply not true. Take, for example, the situation when some important and desired guest is unexpectedly arriving for dinner and you have to ensure that you do a 'good job' hosting him. Only a few hours are left. You quickly examine what there already is at home, think of a menu that can be achieved within the time but would also be up the 'statement' you want to set. Then you quickly get what is needed, start making preparations in the order that is necessary but also do those things together which can be done together. And so on. Do you really think you do not know how to plan?

With your classroom too, you would need to start by finding out where the children already are, where you think they should get to in the time available. What you have to do and the sequence in which you have to do it, and so on.

However, in order to do a 'good job' while the meal is being cooked, you keep checking from time to time whether things are OK or not, whether you have added the salt or things are cooked sufficiently.

This is what ongoing evaluation is like. You keep an eye on whether learning is going in the right direction or not. Similarly, it is crucial to ensure that you make sure things are available where they should be, that time is not wasted and all resources you have are well utilised. This is what, in the big words of academic educationalists, is called 'management' or 'classroom organisation'. In reality, it is something that anyone who has ever hosted a guest (or done hundreds of ordinary everyday tasks) already knows enough about.

At the same time, you do your best to put your guest at ease, to make him feel wanted and cared for. You want to make sure that he feels like coming to your place again! In classroom terms, this would be called a welcome atmosphere, and is one of the key enabling factors that helps learning.

And finally

What this note assumes it is that the teacher is not an 'empty vessel' who has to be told what to do. Instead, the teacher here is regarded as a partner with whom the basic principles need to be shared and agreed with, based on which she or he will find her or his own solutions. And the key question that needs to be addressed is that of 'hosting' children, and of doing one's best to ensure that they learn actively in an encouraging atmosphere. Can it be done? Are you ready? Here's wishing you the very best in this effort!

□

Children's Library in Schools

—Binodanand Jha

The main function of school is the development of children's efficiency in reading, writing, thinking and understanding. Whenever a child is attached to a school then it is expected that he will have ability to know prescribed language, Mathematics, Environment in the curriculum but there are many children in our schools who could not learn reading and writing. How can they read and stick their mind toward studies. ? This problem makes us concerned.

When we talk to children, we get to know their problems and also gather that they only have one or two books. At their home they neither have material and things required nor the congenial atmosphere for studies. Can any child learn through one or two books, available with him? And how will interest be developed? Probably not. When a child reads as many books, sees pictures, discusses, hears and tells stories, reads poems, his efficiency and interest is developed—but how will all this happen?

Its solution to a certain extent is school's library. Here Library does not mean a storage of books or its delivery. Rather it is a programme for reading and studies in which teachers as well as children will feel delighted. This library will not be a burden on teachers but will make his job easier, interesting and result oriented. In this library teachers' work will be in the initial stage. He will organise it with the cooperation of children and the class will run in full depth. Those teachers who have got practical experience of supervising Library will realise how good and important is this work. During the course of work we can have proficiency and ability to supervise a Library.

There are 4 points to be kept in mind:

1. Library should be run with the aim of improving capability of children toward studies.
2. In its supervision full cooperation of boys and girls be taken
3. Books are for children—they should go through them—do activities on them.
4. Books should be kept properly. They should not be kept in bad shape, torn etc., but in case during the course of reading if they are torn—teacher be not held responsible for it.

How to Start

After acquiring the books its formal inauguration should be done in a function in which families of students, teachers, School Education Committee, representatives of Panchayat and Community be invited. In the function a holy message be given that from today Library is formally inaugurated in the school. Every year this day will be celebrated as Library Day.

Management and Maintenance

1. A list of books be prepared in such a manner that students may get books of their liking and interest. For this the list be displayed on a card at a proper place.
2. In the stock register—name of the book writer, publishers and price be mentioned. Following format may be used for that.
   Date Received Writer name Title of book Publisher name yr/place of pub Price

3. Books should be serially numbered as per the stock register.
4. In the beginning books will not be allowed to be taken out. But after some months when the teaching activity is streamlined and stabilised for Sundays and for short duration of vacations books may be allowed to be taken to home.
5. Library Committee be constituted. It should consist of Principal, Teachers, Monitor of Classes and other children.
6. Books will be kept in Box or Almirah. But during Library period they should be kept in such a manner so that children can reach them easily. After the Library period they may again be kept in box or almirah.
7. Rules for issue of books be decided in consultation with the children such as which books will be displayed class wise, for how many days books may be issued for home, what will be the penalty for late return and what will happen if the book is torn at home.
8. Children themselves should take out the books, distribute and later on arrange them

The Use of Library: How?

1. For giving knowledge about the available books in the library an exhibition be arranged in which all the teachers of the school, children, parents and members of School Education Committee be invited. The arrangement and organised manner be attractive so that the children are attracted.
2. In the daily time table as per convenience a period should be allotted to Library.
3. There should be an aim from Library that creates spark among children to collect material from nearby, encouraging inquisitiveness among them.

4. Those Children who could not read should take books with pictures and discuss the subject—this will enable them to be a part of Library.
5. Material which has been read be spoken to children in their own language. Activities and Small Play should be organised.
6. Read books be analysed.
7. Small groups of children be made—to develop their imagination, stories and poems be written by them covering Cat, Dog, Rat and Car etc.
8. Children be encouraged to write Stories and Poems by seeing pictures, incidents.
9. A book be identified in library and children be asked to locate that.
10. In the Library related games on a certain page be identified where mixed words are there.
11. Children may be asked to say dialogue in the book in their own way. They can be asked to play different roles
12. A number of activities are to be explored which make the library purposeful to children.
13. Any news in the News Paper be pasted on the Notice Board by a child.
14. Library be so utilised that the Students of first and second class can read with correct pronunciation.
15. Reading on their own, writing, taking decision, experience of creation, arranging things be inculcated in children through Library.
16. Book Fair on fortnightly, monthly basis can be a good model for the success of Library.

Prosperity: How

1. For prosperity of Library important cuttings from news papers be affixed and kept in a file.
2. Creation of children in the form of Poems, Stories be kept in their own handwriting.

3. Every house, city has its own stories. Small form of it can be affixed on card board and displayed.
4. Material to be published through the help of eminent persons, handwritten books be collected.
5. Creation of Library Fund.
6. Collection of Old Books and Magazines.
7. Collection of New Books based on new techniques.
8. Games such as Snake and Ladder on a board be kept at Library.
9. On the Anniversary of Great People and Festivals, special programmes be arranged for poem recitation, plays and dramas by children. Help from locally available Freedom Fighters, Dramatists, Poets, Singers may be taken. Ex students of the school may be helpful.

   When children use a book, it is possible that the book may be torn. There should not be any worry for this. Children after an interval may take up its repair themselves.
10. Every month books should be cleaned—removing dust etc. This work be taken by senior students.
11. Everybody should become part of library movement and should connect children, books and experience with the outer world.

□

Story of a Learner

—**Pushpa Jha**

A lad of 16-17 years named Bindeshwar Kumar got admitted in Inter Vocational Trade MLT (Medical Lab Technician) in the year 2000.

It was the month of early November, advent of winter. I was sitting in the adjacent verandah of the school premises. That place was a bit peaceful and bright sunshine lightly touching the verandah slowly but readily announcing the winter to come and we all lady teachers would spend our time there during our lunch time and free periods. All the registration work (filling the OMR sheet), form fill up, answer book corrections, tabulation of the sent up exams, completing the class register (attendance), all the money collected from the students, meticulously written in each and every column against the names of the students and, finally, calculating the total figure written in each and every column of the register at the end, submitting the money to the head clerk then duly signed by the Principal and stamped were done continuously. In between these works, we used to eat some wafers or lunch brought from home, and would gossip. Actually, we enjoyed the warm soothing sunshine in that verandah throughout winter.

Sometimes, I was alone sitting, musing gloomily or writing letters to my daughter who was away studying at IIT Roorkee.

I can conclude that lot of work done like formulating questions for Science Quiz, preparing students for the National Anthem and other patriotic songs for 15th August and 26th January; helping them making them memorise for the debate etc. in that verandah.

I loved that verandah, sitting there and looking at the flowers, filled my mind with delicate and tender ideas.

And then one fine morning, from nowhere the boy named Bindeshwar Kumar appeared before me and sat near my feet, touched my feet with great reverence and started introducing himself and then told me that he had enquired and came to know that I was a Biology teacher.

He started pleading me with folded hands, that "please Madam, teach me something" so that he would be able to stand, get educated and could earn as little as to make his two ends meet.

I was startled to see his confidence. He took over me and explained that there was no MLT teacher, he had been jailed.

One thing I did not mention earlier that the classrooms along that verandah belonged to Inter-vocational and Inter-science faculty. There was no tradition of taking of Inter-vocational classes. Vocational teachers would come by noon. They would open their room and for two three hours talked and had some lunch and then by 3 o'clock they would lock the door and would leave. Everything regarding vocational course was on papers. Every year students would get admitted, fill forms and appear in the examination. Vocational instructor would give them very good marks in all the laboratory works (by taking some favours from the students). Students would pass MLT, Electronics, Computer, Accountancy with good marks without even understanding the trade in which they had passed. I doubt even the instructors themselves bothered to understand anything. This was the sordid affair going on. Principals would come and go but they never dared to interfere. Some Principals would become great friends and always helped them gain monetarily. This was the norm nobody would question. No students, Administration and Secondary teachers would pay a heed to those instructors as if they were not the part of the curriculum.

Bindeshwar Kumar used to come to school everyday; would stand in the prayer and would touch the feet of each and every teacher, peons, Principal without fail. All the peons would make fun of him. Bindeshwar Kumar was a very ordinary-looking adolescent, dark, thin, small eyes, high cheek bones, flat nose, and reddish brown erect hair. He somewhat looked malnourished as half the Indians look alike. He belonged to no archives, no tradition at all. Most of the time, he would look inadequate, very conspicuous among the urban children. He was very poor, naïve and gullible. It seemed that perhaps he felt like misplaced in the school environment, but his confidence and will power to get educated were incomparable. If anybody would praise his determination, a faint smile would catch everybody's eyes, twinkling eyes, white sparkling teeth were very prominent, the glimpse of youth had slowly taken place, which would turn him into a hidden attractive person.

Everyday he would come near me, touch my feet and pray that I should teach him. I was quite irritated by his interference. He was recalcitrant and pressurised me to look at him and should ask him about his studies.

I could not understand what to do. I tried my best to get rid of him, but failed utterly.

One day I was formulating questions for the Quiz contest which was to be held at Science College.

Dr. N. Sinha, HOD, Zoology Department, R.U. had procured a project from 'Directorate of Science & Technology', Delhi.

Project was on developing a student's interest towards taking Science at the graduation level instead of pursuing Engineering and Medicine. She was 'Contact Scientist' for the project. She contacted class eleven science students from the prestigious schools as a participant in the seven-day workshop to be held at Science College.

She contacted me for choosing and collecting the names of students. She had nominated me as a resource person for the programme.

I liked the programme very much. I was working intensively towards the interaction of the students. I had created a number of programme like Debate, Science Quiz, Science Exhibition, etc.

Young boys and girls were very enthusiastic and were taking part in each and every programme vigorously. Eminent scientists, professor, doctors, engineers from different Universities & Institutions were giving Power Point presentations and trying to influence the students to pursue different courses, all related to various scientific fields. They successfully gave guidance and counselled each and every student to pursue pure science, other than engineering and medicine. Future belongs to pure science and there is no dearth of opportunity in other fields of science. For that, proper aptitude and innovative ideas are important. Students should come forward and should not get frustrated. The programme was a huge success and excitement level was at its peak. Students were discussing fearlessly with eminent scholars and in that heightened atmosphere, this Bindeshwar Kumar persuaded me like anything to take him as a participant from my school. I had no words to express my embarrassment.

I was disgusted but my Principal somehow convinced me to take him with me. I had already chosen my two good students to participate in the workshop. Bindeshwar Kumar was extra. Altogether, 32 students from different schools, two students from each school were allowed.

I had three students with me. Madam Sinha looked at Bindeshwar with amusement and a smile. She nodded her head with affirmation and told me not to get embarrassed and let him participate. Actually, she was startled to sense his feeling and sheer confidence. He was very-very happy to get included, eyes were twinkling with joy and he smiled at me. He had proved himself victorious. He was courageous, having no inhibition and mingled well with those students from the elite schools.

He used to listen carefully and sincerely and whatever he could understand, he wrote in his note-book. Madam Sinha was very sympathetic towards him, specially calling his name in all the activities; always enquiring about his breakfast and lunch. Within two to three days, he got fully assimilated with the environment. A child is the product of his inherent potential and the environment in which he thrives. If the intrinsic quality is very high, he can imbibe a good intellectual environment immediately. The influence of poor environment cannot diminish his potential.

The boy was discovering himself. Now I could understand the vision of Dr. Sinha Side by side, research was being carried out in the field of Pedagogy. How a person of high potential subjected to the completely new environment can reinvent himself with no time! On the fourth day of the workshop, a Science Quiz was organised. Students were seriously preparing for the contest. Bindeshwar Kumar asked me for help. Again I was annoyed. He requested me that he would also participate in the Quiz competition. I could not gather any courage to stop him. I was ashamed and felt sorry for him.

Then I asked him if he could learn by heart some biological names of species. He earnestly agreed and vanished away from my sight.

Finally, the 'Science Quiz' started with all fanfare.

There were four groups, eight students in each group. He was an odd man, but one of the group's students whom he had befriended generously agreed to take him in his group. The Quiz started. It was quite eventful and extravagant.

Quiz Master was asking questions in different categories and passing the questions from one group to another if the group who had to answer could not answer. If nobody could answer, then I would come on the stage and answer the question and also explain the concept. It was highly appreciated. Suddenly, Quiz master asked the Biological names of some species.

Surprisingly, no one could answer. Bindeshwar Kumar stood up and answered with all confidence. Audience was surprised to hear that the answers were right.

Nobody could imagine the boy had turned around the enormous stone of ignorance. He had surely achieved something which was very new to him.

He was declared Quiz Master. His team had won!

On the last day of the workshop, students had made their Science Model and had arranged for exhibition. Many erudite people had been invited. They were very keen to understand the concept of the model from the students. Students had laboured hard and they were anxiously waiting for the Education Minister to visit the exhibition. Honourable Minister was the Chief Guest and he had to decide the best exhibit. Bindeshwar Kumar had no inkling for this kind of model-making or anything like that. Again he came to me and asked for help. I had said to him that it was impossible for him to take part in this event. With all irritation, I had told him to make the models of Evolution of Man which was printed on the backside of his Science book. He was just like that 'Early man' I had remarked at him. But he took my suggestion as eagerly as always. Perhaps he had found love of a mother who always scolds her son for his incapability but actually, she always wants her son to win.

I was amazed to see his model on a cardboard. With the help of thermocol he had made all the models from 'Homo erectus' to 'Homo hobilous' to 'early man' to 'Homo sapiens' (modern thinking man). Honourable Minister too was amazed to see the boy. He was so different from other students. But then, he had tried his best to show his talent. All the models were well crafted, names were written with sketch pen on a small piece of paper, and with the help of a pin, they were flagged. The boy's endeavour was heart-rendering. Each and every person was praising him with moist eyes. Honourable Minister declared his exhibit the best one. He won lots of prizes and was considered the best participant for his hard work.

He made his own luck.

But looking at success, there is an alternative to luck, synchronicity.

Synchronicity is the ability to create good luck and find invisible support from nowhere that would make anybody a leader in any field.

The boy had made an impact in a very short time among the elite students. That was his ultimate ability to connect.

Madam Sinha gave a pat on his back with a smile.

I understood that our children face fear, anxiety, anger and pain in their life. Especially, teachers should tell them that they love their students and accept them unconditionally, whatever be their condition and whatsoever be the results. Children should feel secure and confident. Teachers should always talk with a smile and a word of encouragement would pay rich dividend later on in the pupil's life. A teacher should be as humble as grass. When we let go of perfection, allow ourselves to do things imperfectly, come to see how perfect we are just the way we are.

Everybody should understand that the child's need can't wait. We are guilty of many errors and many faults but our worst crime is abandoning the children, neglecting the fountain of life. Many of the things we need can wait, a child can't. To him, we cannot answer "tomorrow". His name is "today".

Great Philosopher, teacher and President of India, S. Radhakrishnan had said, "The end product of education should be a free creative man who can battle against historical circumstances and adversities of nature."

A teacher affects his students to the eternity.

"Happy Teachers' Day"

□

One Who could not See Despite Seeing

—Hellen Killer

Hellen Killer (1880-1968, America) is such a name which provides light within a great and grave darkness. Imagine one who can neither hear nor see but can Learn reading—writing and speaking, live a life full of aspirations, whose contribution to the World become memorable. It was - Hellen Killer. When she was one and half year old due to a serious illness she lost her vision and hearing ability, but she never took it as a defeat. In her Autobiography named "Story of Life" published during her College days she wrote "I don't remember how it happened but it was why night is not ending and morning is not seen. This book has been translated in all the languages of the World. Apart from this 10 books and hundreds of articles written by her are published. She travelled entire world to canvass for rights of people like herself and for World's peace. Hellen also came to India.

She viewed

Sometimes I take test of my friends so as to know what they see. Recently a beloved friend of mine came back after touring Forest. I asked her 'WHAT YOU HAVE SEEN THERE'.

'Nothing very specific' was her reply. I was not very surprised as I am used to such type of answers. It is my belief that those who have eyes see very less.

Whether it is possible that one who walk in the forest for one hour could not see any thing. To me who can not see—hundreds of interesting things are there which I recognise by touching them. I can differentiate the Bhoj Patra and Cheed tree by touching their trees. During Autum I search for new buds. I am amazed when I touch flowers. It is like a magic by nature. When I am fortunate and put my hand on – flower-a bird starts singing. I am delighted to touch flowing water of a stream. I like Cheed leaves than costly Carpets. Sometimes my heart has a wish to see all these fascinating things. I feel that when only by touching – then I am so happy—what will happen when I could have seen them. But those who have eyes definitely see very less. The different colour of This World are not having any impact on their conscious. Man never admires their capabilities. He always aspires for a thing which is not with him.

It is a matter of pain that the blessing of vision is considered to be a normal thing whereas this blessing can fill your life with seven colours of happiness.

□

How Children Learn

—**Binodanand Jha**

1. All Children are capable to learn and as a nature are prone to learn.
2. All Children can learn if they are allowed to adopt their own pace.
3. Learning is a continuous process. So learning is not restricted to the school but is beyond the boundary of school as well. Thus a connection is to be maintained between Class and Home.
4. Children usually learn when they play or work.
5. Children learn among them.
6. Art prepares a basis for learning.
7. Children learn by experience, by preparing things, by reading, by experimenting, by asking, by discussing etc.
8. Mistakes are committed by children during learning. In fact mistakes are important source for learning.
9. Children learn in continuity and not in pieces. For example when you are reading these written words they are read in entirety, and not by breaking in words, etc.
10. Children themselves construct their knowledge. They do not wait for teachers or elders to speak – something for writing.
11. Children confirm by repeating acquired knowledge.

□

Requirement of Children with Special Needs

Children who are not able to see as the normal or having a vision level of 6/6 needs special requirements to be attended. Depending upon their impairment many stages have been suggested

Generally such children need assistance for going to school from their home. They also need help for reaching into Class Room, reading written directions and for writing. For example, if they are the Children in whom disability is less—books with bigger or enlarged font be made available to them but when disability is more brail or speaking books be made available. In case these are not available, audio cassettes may be used. Available material within our environment also may be used. Gopi is a student. He almost sits in the last row and is not able to write what Teacher has written on Black Board. After some days when he was placed in first row – is now able to write correctly and neatly in the Exercise Book. Have you experienced such examples in your Class?

There is one challenge before you as to how class can be changed for almost zero vision (Drishtibadhit) children.

Here are some methods through which we can make the school congenial to the required environment:

- Class Room should have sunlight so that children can see Black Board and Teacher.

- Doors and Furniture should not have sharp edges. Knells should be properly inside.
- When children talk they should first tell their name. This helps impaired Children to recognise them and they can participate in talks.
- Assisting material should be used so that impaired/ disabled children can realise them by hearing, touching and experiencing. For example if food items are discussed in the Class room then there can be a box containing spices, there can be different types of vegetables or foods or there can be their models.
- It is necessary for a teacher to speak loudly what he has written on the Board so that disabled children feel themselves to be in Group.
- Most of the work be done in small groups.
- School should have facility of Medical assistance.
- Source of Education be in Braille.
- All children should link solution of their problem with real life problems and debate on them be encouraged.
- In the environment of contemporary education different methods such as symbolic small works, touch and understand be used.
- Every teacher should be trained in Special Education. To make a school all inclusive it is very necessary.

Difficulties of Children having Impaired Hearing

- Not able to hear.
- Few can hear partially.
- Use of hearing Machine.
- Not able to speak clearly.
- Unclear speaking.
- Not able to hear feeble voice.
- For communication use of symbols.

Difficulties of Mentally Retarded Child

- Because of less average mind dullness in physical and mental activities.
- Not able to recognise normal creature.
- Finding difficulty in drawing or even hand writing.
- Not able to concentrate on any type of activity.
- Not capable to take part in sports meant for the same age group.
- Preference to sit with younger children.
- Showing hesitation in activities.

Difficulties of Children Suffering from Disability in Movement

- No control on body.
- Lack of Control on entire body.
- Continuous tension or stiffness in muscles.
- Proper seating arrangement for them in the Class.

Peculiarities of Disabled Children

- As regards brain they may be equal to normal children may be less or more than them.
- Such children experience difficulty in recognizing certain words.
- They may read' in place of 'b'.
- They may write q in place of p.
- They may make mistake by taking 6 in place of 9, 69 in place of 96.
- Such children generally are not able to concentrate on their work.
- They sometimes react without thinking.
- Such children quickly get worried.
- They are not able to concentrate on any work for long.
- Ups and downs are evident in their status.
- They experience doubts.

Desirable Changes to be Made in Class Room for Disabled Children

What changes should be carried out. A teacher should ensure to provide opportunity to disabled children for learning. It is necessary that we should not ignore peculiar requirements and to make all out effort for meeting their requirement and boost their moral.

□

Evaluation

Traditional Evaluation

1. Done once or twice in a year.
2. It is expected from all the students that they would learn within 3 months or within prescribed period. Their style and speed totally ignored.
3. Pressure is there on the teacher to complete course within prescribed period.
4. This is based on memorising.
5. Limited in nature. Importance is given to Text Books.
6. Formal and artificial.
7. Great importance to Mistakes.
8. Students ability to study is verified.
9. Children have to keep full year course in memory—a great burden.
10. Division/grade are allotted as per mark, a minor difference may cause down grading.
11. Examinations are restricted to pass` or fail. One mark may cause wastage of efforts made during the year.
12. Mostly evaluation is done by outsiders.

Continuous and Comprehensive Evaluation

1. Done continuously throughout the year
2. Children's individual different capabilities are taken into account positively. They are allowed to learn as per their speed.

3. Teachers have got freedom to change teaching methods in accordance with the interest and ability of Students.
4. Evaluation is done on the basis of understanding behaviour and continuous viewpoint.
5. It is broad-instead of bookish knowledge behavioural changes and their own knowledge are important.
6. Informal-attached to daily life.
7. It is centered on the efficiency of a child – effort made to remove mistakes.
8. Not only students' but teachers' proficiency is also examined.
9. Not necessary to keep all the things in memory. It provides opportunity to understand since pressure is less.
10. Grades more preferred than numbers. There are less possibility of tension and jealousy.
11. The purpose of this is not only to recognise the abilities but also the progress since continuous evaluation is there they get opportunity to improve.
12. It is a part within during continuous evaluation.

□

Some Indicators of Quality Education

1. Opening and closure of school on time.
2. Conducting Morning Assembly on time.
3. All teachers and children be on time—punctual in attending School.
4. Every Child and every Teacher engrossed in the process of teaching and learning.
5. Teacher to have knowledge of child's educational level.
6. Continuous and overall evaluation.
7. For Class-I a full time teacher.
8. Full use of Black Boards in all the Classes.
9. Daily Time Table to be displayed in all the classes.
10. Last period should be for Sports, Arts and Cultural Activities.
11. Use of available story books, sports material.
12. Serving of Mid Day Meal as per menu.
13. Active Children's Parliament and Meena Manch.
14. Children in clean cloth and clean school.
15. Use of facility of Drinking water and Lavatories.
16. Plantation in school premises.
17. Proper use of grants received.
18. All children should have their own text books.
19. In the meeting of school education committee regular discussion on qualitative education.
20. Regular parents-teachers class wise meeting.

□

Duties and Responsibilities of School and its Stakeholders

Environment in the school plays an important role in the learning process of the children. Neat and Clean atmosphere and fearless premises of the School encourage them to Study. School's atmosphere should be in consonance with children's liking and for this children's participation ought to be enhanced. Children are the centre of this entire movement, so in every school in the school management committee, parents, teachers and principal will have to decide certain things/issues and then there should not be any compromise on them. For this, functions and responsibilities are decided for all levels.

Functions and Responsibilities of School

1. Every school should commence and close at the prescribed time.
2. In the afternoon there should be a session for Thinking.
3. Time Table be prepared, pasted or affixed in all the Classes.
4. Information about Present and absent students be placed daily on Notice Board.
5. Black Board should be there in all the Classes.
6. Mid day meal should be as per parameter and Menu.
7. Children's Parliament be constituted.

8. Middle Schools should have Meena Manch.
9. For Class-I a special teacher be nominated and from 2nd to 4th, teacher for Mathematics and Language be nominated.
10. Text Books, Story Books and Sport Material etc., be made available to every Child.
11. Development of Sports, Arts and Culture be made part of everyday's Curriculum.
12. Basic amenities be ensured, for example, pure and clean drinking water, lavatories. All the class rooms be utilised.
13. Progress of the children be made known to Parents.

Teacher's Function and Responsibility

1. Teachers should not remain absent.
2. Teacher should study all text books of his class.
3. Teachers should know Educational Level of particularly Class-I and Class-VIII.
4. Teacher should use TLM.
5. Every Child's Educational Achievement be known to teacher.
6. Teachers should tell the progress of children to their parents weekly.
7. Progress in Achievement Level be entered in the Register and it be shown to parents.
8. Teachers by taking interest teach students and plan for next days teaching.
9. Ensure or make effort for Students attending school regularly.

Functions and Responsibilities of Principal

In the administration of school principal has got an important role to play. Principals are not there in the Primary School. The senior teacher act as Principal. Whether Principal or senior teacher – they have to prepare plan for the supervision of teaching and School.

Principal will have following Functions

1. To ensure teacher's presence and punctuality
2. With the assistance of teachers make plan for improving achievement levels of Students
3. To know the standard of children through teachers and to set goal in accordance with that.
4. For Class-I a special teacher be nominated who should teach Language and Mathematics and other teachers should teach other subjects.
5. Principal should also teach like a teacher in the class.
6. To ensure regular parents-teacher meeting.
7. To cooperate teachers in finding solution to the problems faced by them.
8. To meet teachers regularly for assessing work plan.
9. To ensure regular attendance of teachers.

Functions and Responsibilities of Parents

1. To meet Principal/Teacher to know the progress of their child.
2. To attend Parents-Teacher Meeting and contribute through suggestions for improving achievement level of children.
3. To discuss benefits of such movements in home, mohalla, kasba for creating a positive environment.

Functions and Responsibilities of VSS/SMC

As per Right to Education Act, Education Committee is to be constituted in every school. In the Act the responsibility of VSS/SMC are elaborately dealt with. Along with those VSS/SMC may acquire following responsibilities in connection with this proposed Movement.

1. To encourage parents for sending their children to school.
2. To invite members of children's Parliament/Meena Manch in the meeting of VSS.

3. Spend School Development Grant judiciously.
4. To ensure progress and adequate participation of dejected children.
5. During the visit of Coordinator make him aware of the problems relating to Studies.

Functions and Responsibilities of Coordinators

1. To visit every school twice a month for providing academic support.
2. To assist teachers in (a) continuous and comprehensive overall evaluation of children,(b) stage of educational achievement.
3. To verify children's achievement.
4. To inspect the register containing entries regarding level of teaching during tour.
5. Agenda to be made before one day training programme.
6. Continuous overall evaluation of teachers.
7. To discuss hurdle faced by teachers
8. If academic problems of the teacher are not solved, they be taken up with District Institute of Education and Training (DIET) through block resource centre for solution.
9. To ensure use of Books in Library, sports material and other available items through discussion with Principal.
10. During visit – to oversee Parents-Teachers Meeting and to meet parents
11. To submit report to the distt. Coordinator in the prescribed format.
12. To encourage Principal on behalf of school management
13. Informing in detail regarding steps taken for quality education to the representatives Of panchayat Mukhia/ward members.

14. To dwell upon parameters prescribed by Education Deptt., their classification and to verify its registers.
15. To take stock of all the statistics, figures of school.

Functions and Responsibilities of District Level Officers/Functionaries

1. To ensure visit of any Sadhansevi to all the Schools of District within 3 months.
2. For examining academic support by BRP—visit to be made to school.
3. To act as academic thread between school and DIET/SCERT.
4. To give responsibility to the Sadhansevi regarding monitoring of schools.
5. To form a Distt. Level Resource Group consisting of Educationist, Representative of panchayat and community who from time to time shall visit schools and evaluate progress made there.
6. On the basis of visits to the School prepare plan for Coordinator.
7. Encourage Coordinator of Resource Centre.
8. To help teacher during monthly visits.
9. Get Visit Report from Sadhansevi and to include it in BIC.
10. To submit report in the prescribed format on progress of campaign to Distt. Administration on regular interval.
11. Full briefing be given to representative of panchayat/committee.
12. Monthly visit by BRP of at least 10 schools.
13. To clarify Sankul as per the parameters prescribed in Bihar Education Qualitative Mission and to keep full knowledge of it.

□

Human Development

India's more than half population is young. Human Development is only possible when younger generation and children can develop their entire capability. Mission Human Development will be successful only when special initiatives are taken for education, health, nourishment, sanitation, cleanliness, social justice, women empowerment, mahadalit, very backward and minorities. For taking country ahead Mission Human Development is to be taken as a people's movement. Schools will be in the centre of this movement. From time to time through conducting Social Festivals efforts will be made to connect schools with society—to bring them near. Our schools will become Centre for social changes and our children will be soldiers for taking the Society on a developing path. Children can become leader for crusade against social evils (dowry, child marriages, sex determination, use of tobacco, dishonesty etc). School can be made the centre for social changes along with knowledge, expertise and lively education.

Following are required to be spread among house to house for Mission Human Development:

1. All children should regularly acquire life's education in the school.
2. Girls be not married before 18 years and the paucity of blood in them be removed.
3. In the New Generation Health Guarantee Programme boys of 0-14 years and girls of 0-18 years be medically

checked every year and treatment if required be given.

4. To avoid disease – cleanliness be ensured in villages and Swachhta Abhiyan be undertaken.
5. Pure and clean Drinking water can save us from disease.
6. Newly born babies to have mother's milk for at least 6 months.
7. In all villages and localities treatment for children shall be made available on time, so that no child suffer from malnutrition.
8. Through Anganwadi Centres specially the height, weight of Child from 0-3 years be measured so that malnutrition is checked.
9. Literacy Programme for female of mahadalit, minorities and very backward be conducted at schools-so that they can become literate mother's.
10. Tobacco and liquor are dangerous for health. Survey can be conducted through children.
11. Activity for plantation be taken so that atmosphere remains clean.
12. Activities of Regular Sports, Yoga and Dhyan for Children.
13. Girls specially be encouraged to study in Higher Schools.
14. Along with development of expertise women's saving group be also formed.
15. Positive thinking, regard and respect to the labour and discipline in life for physical values be encouraged. Mission Manav Vikas Centers be established in school with a view to make the mission a centre point. This should be made attractive by putting posters, pictures, models designed by children. During school festivals, children should take their parents a round of it explaining its importance. During Inter school competition best corner may be awarded.

□

Motivational Short Stories

Voice of Truth

Bankei was a great Jain Guru—when he passed away, thousands of disciples assembled. Among them one was blind who was telling continuously that Bankei really was a great man. Somebody asked him how you can see this with so much of confidence. The blind replied that "I am not learned, cannot see. But still I can deeply listen to the voice of many people which may not be picked up by those who have got eyes. For me his voice is the only medium which provides me clue to distinguish him to others. When I hear somebody greeting the other I can hear the feeling of jealousy also. When somebody met with an accident and other console him I find the voice of happiness and satisfaction. But for so many years Bankei's voice always talked of truth. When he expressed happiness there was truth and nothing else and when he expressed grief, it was grief only

This in fact is our story. With little honesty we should examine our thoughts. We will see that what we are telling is not what we are experiencing. Our Heart, its liking is very jealous. Misfortune is that the same is developed and reaped in by our Education and family atmosphere. From the childhood it has never been taught how we should feel happy in other's happiness. It is like that life is a competition where one's success is dependent on other's failure. Man has become two facet, he has got two faces. To show one but the real is the other one.

What is tension? It is the tussle between these two. This tussle makes your mind sick and you feel loneliness because you cannot reach to anybody.

Yardstick for Decency and Gentleness

Swami Vivekanand in his Saint attire was going on a road in the Chicago City. His dress was subject of curiosity for Americans. A lady behind him remarked to her male friend see the unique dress of this gentleman.

Swamijee heard that and told that woman 'Madam, in your Country tailors are known as manufactures of Culture and the Clothes are yardstick for courtesy but the Country from where I have come—a man is known and recognised by his character.

The lady felt ashamed of her remarks.

Education through Lines

When Swami Ramteerth was a Professor. One day he drew a line on the Black Board and asked the students to make it short without wiping it. One intelligent boy got up and made another line bigger than that—successfully making the earlier one short without wiping.

This made Ramteerth glad and he said "Students, this process may be used by you in your life. If you want to become big you should not throw others back. You should do big works and become big. Then others automatically will become small.

Effect of Sweat Particles

When Bhagwan Ram went to meet Shabari he saw all the flowers were full of blossoms—none of them was dried. There was great fragrance coming out of them. He asked with curiosity the reason for the same. Shabari said "God ! behind this there is a story. Long back here was the ashram of Rishi Matang. Many Rishis and Students used to reside here. Before rainy season the available coal etc. was about to exhaust. It was necessary to store them before rains. Due to lethargy the students did not go to bring wood. One day aged Matang Rishi himself went to bring woods. When they saw the Guru going students also joined him. Dry woods were cut and soon they were back on the way to Ashram. He Ram! Impact of great labour was evident on the body of Guru. Students were also sweating. Where ever the shrambindu (sweat) of Rishi fell these beautiful flowers grew up and then they are in the entire forest. It is his pious effect that they are still fresh. Meaning thereby that the work done with good intention spreads fragrance and can flourish on soil.

The Result of Politeness

At one time Chinese Saint Chang Chuang fell ill. Laatse visited him and requested for some preaching. Chang Chuang asked him why a person visiting his village gets down from Car. Laatse replied—this tradition means that the man should not forget his roots.

Then Chang opened his mouth and asked, "Are there teeth in my mouth? Laatse replied 'no' and 'tounge',—Chang asked. Laatse said, 'yes, it is.' Chang asked, 'why so?' Can you tell me the reason? Sir, my view is that as tongue is soft it has remained but teeth being hard have vanished. Chang replied with satisfaction. " You have replied correctly. It is good to be polite and soft. I am confident that you have learnt all the principles of World and no preaching is required for you.

Resolution

Student asked – Teacher Sir! Who's rule is on stone? Teacher replied 'of iron'. Student again asked, "And on Iron?" Teacher replied 'of Fire'. Student's next question was 'and on Fire' teacher replied 'of Air'. Student again asked – there may be somebody's rule on Air. Guru told, yes, why not, Resolution is having rule on Air. Before the man's Resolution Power air becomes small and tiny. We should take resolution that we will love ourselves, love our school and our children, will provide them the opportunity to develop.

Risk

One farmer is sowing seeds in his agricultural field. Definitely he is taking risk. If rain does not help, his money is going to be wasted. Somebody asks him "Why are you taking risk, why don't you sell it playing safe?" The farmer replied, those who don't take risk will not be able to move ahead.

Work

No work is small but the person doing that treat and term it small or big. Every work is important and it should be done with full dedication. Work done half heartedly always remains incomplete causing tension. Also remember that no work is difficult rather its beginning is difficult.

Among the Children

After long tiredness to reenergise your self is an art. Many a time after long tiredness, we prefer to sit idle anticipating that it will recharge us. This way body gets rest but not the mind. The greatest Tennis Champion Novan Jokowitch never prefers to sit idle. He spends time with children—those who have to learn walking. He says children help me remain tension free. I get energy from them which provides me relief from tiredness.

This may be his own way. Our method may be different from them. In fact no healthy man can be suffering from tension. He always remains energetic. On mental level we are sick when mind does not get relief. There are many ways to get relief. Children as they are more near to nature, their august company, keeps us natural. The creator of Panchtantra - Acharya Vishnu Sharma was also seeking such august company. He learnt writing among them, while playing with them, knowing their habits he wrote the Panchtantra. It is not that we don't spend time like this but yes we do not feel it necessary.

Ex-President APJ Kalam despite his preoccupations never forgot to be with children. In them he was seeing his past and Country's future. He was filling their liveliness in himself. He was convinced that without taking them nothing can be done. After all he lived as he wanted to. We can also make such efforts.

□

National Anthem, Rashtrageet and Some Poems

1. Rashtragaan

Jan-gan-man adhinayak jay hey,
Bharat bhagya vidhata.
Punjab, Sindh, Gujarat-Maratha
Dravid-Utkal-Bang.
Vindhya, Himachal, Yamuna, Ganga
Uchchhal jaladhi Taranga
Tav shubh name jaage
Tav shubh aashish mange
Gahe tav jai gatha.
Jan-gan mangal dayak jai he
Bharat bhagya vidhata
Jay he, jay he, jay he
Jay, jay, jay jay he

2. Rashtrageet

Vande matram! Vande matram!
Sujalam, suphlam, malayaj sheetlam
Sashya shyamlam, matram!vande matram

Shubhra-jyotsnam pulkit yaminim
phoolla kusumita drumdal shobhinim
Suhasinim, sumadhur bhasinim

Sukhdam, vardam matram
Vande matram!vande matram!

3. Bihar Geet

Mere Bharat ke kanth-haar
Tujhko shat-shat vandan Bihar.
Tu valmiki ki Ramayan
Tu vaishali ka loktantra
Tu bodhisattva ki karuna hai
Tu mahavir ka shanti mantra
Tu nalanda ka gyandeep
Tu hi akshat chandan Bihar

Tu hai ashok ki dharamdhwaja
Tu guru govind ki vani hai
Tu aryabhatt, tu shershah
Tu kunwarsigh balidani hai
Tu bapu ki hai karmabhumi
Dharti ka nandan van Bihar

Teri gaurav gatha apurva
Tu vishwa shanti ka agradoot
Lautega khoya swabhiman
Aaj jag chuke tere sapoot
Ab tu mathe ka vijay tilak
Tu ankho ka anjan Bihar
Tujhko shat – shat vandan Bihar.
Mere Bharat ke kanth-haar!!!!

4. Bihar Rajya Prarthna

Meri raftar par suraj ki kiran naaz kare
Aisi awaj de malik ki gagan naaz kare
Vah nazar de ki karu kadr harek mazhab ki
Vah mohabbat de mujhe amno aman naaz kare
Meri khushboo se mahak jaye yah dunia malik
Mujhko vo phool bana saara chaman naaz kare

Ilm kuch aisa de mai kaam sabo ke aaun
Hausla aisa hi de gang zaman naaz kare
Aadhe raste par na ruk jae musafir ke kadam
Shauk manzil ka ho itna ki thakan naaz kare.
Deep se deep jalae ki chamak uthe Bihar
Aesi khoobi de ke malik chaman naaz kare
Jai Bihar, Jai Bihar, jai jai jai Bihar

5. Daya Kar Dan Bhakti ka

Dya kar dan bhakti ka, hame parmatma dena
Daya karna hamari atma me shudhta dena.
Hamare dhyan me aao, prabhu ankho me bas jao
Andhere dil me aakar ke, param jyoti jaga dena
Baha do prem ki ganga, dilo me prem ka sagar
Hame aapas me miljulkar, prabhu rahna sikha dena
Hamara dharma ho seva, hamara karma ho seva
Sada iman ho seva vah sevak jan bana dena.
Watan ke vaste jeena, watan ke vaste marna
Watan pe jan fida karna, prabhu hamko sikha dena

6. Hey Prabho Anand data Gyan Hamko Dijiye

He prabho anand data gyan hamko dijiye
Sheeghra sare durguno ko door hamase kijiye
Lijiye apne Sharan me ham sadachari bane
Brahmachari dharma rakshak veer vrat dhari bane.
Ninda ham kisi ki bhi bhool se bhi na karen
Divya jeewan ho hamara, tere yash gaya karen
Prem se hum gurujano ki, nitya hi seva karen
Satya bolen, jhoot tyagen, mel aapas me rahen

7. Tu Hi Ram Hai Tu Rahim

Tu hi Ram hai, tu Rahim hai
Tu karim, Krishna, khuda hua
Tu hi vahe guru, tu yishu masih
Har naam me tu sama raha
Teri jaat pak quran me

Tera daras ved puran me
Guru granth ji ke bakhan me
Tu prakash apna dikha raha
Tu hi Ram hai..........
Ardas hai kahi kirtan
Kahi Ramdhun kahi Aavahan
Vidhi bhed ka yeh sab rachan
Tera bhakt tujhko bula raha
Tuhi Ram tuhi Rahim hai
Tu Karim, Krishna, khuda hua.

8. Anek Roop Me Ek

Har desh me tu, har vesh me tu
Tere naam anek, tu ek hi hai.
Teri rangbhoomi, yeh vishwa dhara
Sab khel me, mel me, tu hi to hai.
Sagar se utha badal banakar
Badal se gira jal ho kar ke
Fir nahar bana, nadia gahri
Tere bhinna prakar, tu ek hi hai
Mitti se anu parmanu bana
Tune divya jagat ka roop lia
Fir parvat vriksha vishal bana
Saundrya tera, tu ek hi hai

9. Desh Ki Mati Desh Ka Jal

Desh ki mati, desh ka jal
Hawa desh ki, desh ke phal
Saras bane prabhu, saras bane.
Desh ke ghar aur desh ke ghat
Desh ke van aur desh ke vat
Saral bane prabhu, saral bane
Desh ke tan aur desh ke man
Desh ke ghar ke bhai-behan
Vimal bane prabhu, vimal bane
Desh ki iccha, desh ki aasha

Kaam desh ke, desh ki bhasha
Ek bane prabhu, ek bane
Desh ki mati, desh ka jal
Hava desh ki, desh ke phal
Saras bane prabhu, saras bane

10. Prabhu Mera Jeevan Ho Sundar

Tan ho sundar, man ho sundar
Prabhu mera jiwan ho sundar
Jagna sundar, sona sundar
Ghar ka kona kona sundar
Prabhu mera aangan ho sundar
Tan ho sundar, man ho sundar
Kapde sundar, khana sundar
Vani sundar, gana sundar
Prabhu mera bachpan ho sundar
Tan ho sundar, man ho sundar
Din ho sundar, raten ho sundar
Sab ho meri baate sundar
Prabhu mera kshan kshan ho sundar
Prabhu mera jeevan ho sundar

11. Man Vijay Kare

Hamko man ki shakti dena man vijay kare
Dusron ki jai se pahle khud ki jai karen.
Bhed bhav apne dil se saaf kar saken,
doston se bhool ho to maaf kar saken
Jhoot se bache rahe, sach ka dam bharen
Dusron ki jai....... !!
Mushkilen pade to hum par itna karam kar,
saath de to dharm ka, chalen to dharm par!!
Khud par hosla rahe, badi se na daren
Dusron ki jai.........!!

12. Itni Shakti Hame Dena Data

Itni shakti hame dena data
Man ka vishwas kamjor ho na!!
Ham chale nek raste par hamse,
Bhul kar bhi koi bhool ho na!!

Door gyan ke ho andhere,
Tu hame gyan ki roshni de.
Har burai se bachte rahe ham,
Jitni bhi de bhali jindagi de!!
Bair ho na kisi ka kisi se,
Bhavna man me badle ki ho na!!

Ham na soche hame kya mila hai,
Ham ye soche kiya kya hai arpaan !!
Phool khushin ke baten sabhi ko,
Saab ka jeevan hi baan jaye madhuvan!!
Apni karuna ka jal tu baha ke,
Kar de pawan harek man ka kona

□□□